Under Cover
Death stalks the book dealer

Under Cover

Death stalks the book dealer

Twelve tales of the intrigue, murder, and mayhem, that infect the
rare book world.

F. J. Manasek

Author of:
Uncommon Value. A rare bookdealer's world
and
Collecting Old Maps: The map collector's vade-mecum

MUSEUM STREET PRESS
Norwich, VT 05055-1204
USA

ISBN 0-9649000-7-6

First edition 1997

This work is fiction. The characters invented for this
work do not have any counterparts in reality. If any such
similarities exist, they are accidental. Real individuals
have been placed in fictitious situations.

Quotations from *The Teaching of Buddha* are courtesy of Bukkyo Dendo Kyokai,
Tokyo, Japan.

Introduction:

Time idle is time dangerous, especially at book fairs. It is here, where once the floor has voided its stream of visitors but fair's end lurks yet in the distance, that time's treadmill slows to an imperceptible pace. And it is during these vulnerable hours that dealers are forced to draw upon their inner resources.

There are some who utilize this time telling wondrous stories of fairs of yore, great book buys past and great sales past. We liken these boasts to that of Admiral Sir John Fisher, First Sea Lord. When Fisher boasted to Edward VII that he had "ravished every virgin in London" the monarch answered, "Splendid, if true."

And, there are those, who, immersed in the bubbling froth of commerce, never cease to scurry back and forth, much like squirrels gathering their winter's cache, working deals and trading books amongst themselves with the ever-hopeful goal of grabbing that rare piece in the corner. We are indebted to these, the titans of bookdealing, for tis 'round them that the fabric of the trade, that ultimate shroud, is woven.

But not we.

Our thoughts, at these fairs, carry us to our earlier lives. Through the clouded cornea of the mind's eye, I revisit the great old days when the numbing Nembutol of trade was offset by keen adventure with as grand and hearty a bunch of chums as any man could have hoped for in this life.

And that has made me indebted to even the dullest of fairs, for their otherwise idle hours, when I can recount those days and put them, for the clear benefit of all posterity, on paper.

Are the episodes in this book true? Is this a *roman à clef?*

You might well ask.

And I answer that *all the words can be documented.* But their sequence has been altered. You will not, however hard you try, be able to recognize the players, with the exceptions of those I wish to identify.

F.J. Manasek
Norwich, Vermont

5

...Prima est haec ultio, quod se
Iudice nemo nocens absolvitur.
— *Juvenal* Satires 13, 1.2

This book is dedicated to those who appear and to those who cannot appear in these reminiscences.

And to those for whom time has stopped.

———

Tarnished is the gold—
with young leaves round us, we look back
to days of old.

— CHORA (1729-1781)

Contents

Under Cover

The Oxford Club

What difference does it make to the dead, the orphans and the homeless, whether the mad destruction is wrought under the name of totalitarianism or the holy name of liberty or democracy?
— Mohandas Karamchand Gandhi *Non-Violence in Peace and War* 1949

I stayed first in the building that is now the Old Parsonage Hotel, on the Banbury Road in Oxford, England, some thirty years ago. In those days, as a residence, it was a lot less *chichi* then it is now, and, in my estimation, a bit more comfortable. There was a largish breakfast area, a space now taken up by several income-producing rooms. The lobby has now been changed extensively and a decorator, a foppish lad, no doubt, has gussied up the place to make it seem, to some, worth four times the old rates. Nonetheless, I continue to go to this wonderful place, built around a 17th-century parsonage. There is now a walled garden in front, shielding it from the passersby, but not the noise, of a busy Oxford street. A true delight of this garden are the dun-colored little birds that swoop down and pick up crumbs from the pavement (Anne calls them Parsonage Swoopers). And, I should not forget the martinis, served from within, made to a perfection not usually found in England, by waiters who are truly competent. Now, after some thirty years and some sixty-plus visits, I feel more than a bit attached to this old building and I am willing to put up with its somewhat dandified interior, that shall, as do all the bezoars of fashion, pass.

My first Oxford winter was difficult. I remember it now, some thirty years later, as an unusually cold one. But perhaps it was just comparatively so. I had left Spain and the wonderful Maria, for what I thought would be only a few weeks. Those weeks turned into months. Maria had cautioned me that this could happen, but cocky, callow lad that I was in those days, I was certain I could finish my assignment and be back with her before long. She and I had long planned to go to Seville and study the archives, and perhaps set out on a trail of adventure following some of the old Spanish explorations in the New World. This never happened; the endless, languid days of our youth played over us without surcease. They had seduced us thoroughly and promised us they would never end. Time for us had stopped. We laughed and played as the days followed each other in splendid, soporific sequence. We let the world pass us by, and we never studied the archives in Seville. Yet even today, we both hold the little unspoken belief within us that we might someday meet in sunny Seville and turn back the clock. I think we can, I think we can pick up our cups of fragrant morning coffee from where we set them down some thirty years ago, drink from that well of youth we never ran dry, and go ahead, together, with our adventure. Perhaps we shall.

And it was from those pleasant days in Madrid with Maria, having been convinced that I could do the job quickly and easily, that I let myself be recruited. With thoughts of a quick return comforting me, I traveled to

Oxford to meet my new colleagues. I was, as Maria already
knew, a fool for flattery.

While the Old Parsonage was my home at night, days
were spent in our cramped laboratory in the bowels of one
of the ancient University buildings, poring over bits and
pieces of data relating to scientific work being carried out
in the Soviet Union. After hours I sipped port, a habit I
have enjoyed to this day, with my friends from work and
play. The ties we established then have lasted 'till now.

My colleagues were mostly Brits. The type so inbred
and highly differentiated that they could communicate by
thought as well as with words. And then there was Lo Ban.
Officially he was Chinese, but we all had our doubts. Lo
Ban, a man of such fluidity that he could assume virtually
any nationality, was daunted only when he tried to pass as
Occidental. Even Lo Ban, the man who reportedly was a
killer as well as a scholar, was limited by phenotype. During
these early meetings Lo Ban said very little and seemingly
contributed not much to our project, but later he proved a
supreme tactician. It was much later, years later, that I
realized just how thorough was the disruption that Lo Ban
wreaked upon our adversaries.

In Oxford, the situation was quickly made apparent.
The Cold War was going strong and parts of it looked bad
for our side. Our regular intelligence agencies could not
provide decent information. At least we thought so. They
of course disagreed, and insisted that we could trust their
data. This was a laughable position since any twenty-year-
old who had backpacked his way across Europe would have
known that their data were wrong. We needed our own

information and we needed it gathered by people who knew what quantitative analysis meant.

The usual people who gathered foreign intelligence for the usual agencies had little capability for thought, let alone rigorous thought. Indeed, most were so mired in their own cultural prejudices that they viewed the world as one large iteration of Reston, Virginia.

Many of the operatives who were most influential in the general arena of "intelligence" were academics from a number of different American universities. It was generally considered, for example, that several major spy centers in the Middle East, set up to eavesdrop on the Soviets, were run by University of Chicago people. The U of C was perfect cover. Known in those days as "the little red schoolhouse" because of the loudly-proclaimed leftist leanings of some of its faculty, this institution, located in Chicago's notorious lower South Side, provided many of the spy-meisters of the period. Who would ever think that these self-proclaimed liberals and leftists would be in the employ of the CIA? And now, some thirty years later, it has been rumored that many were in the employ not only of the CIA, but perhaps were also moonlighting. Seemingly perfect cover. In retrospect, although their cover was good, the quality of their mentation was considerably less than their cover.

Our Side had never been able to get the kind of information we needed about the Soviets' level of expertise in biological and chemical weaponry. The Soviet physical capability was awesome, or so we thought, and it was assumed that their chemical/biological capability was

16

awesome. Assumed is the key word here. Nobody knew. Everybody assumed.

And so it was the Brits who first broke ranks and set up our little group in Oxford.

We needed to know with some certainty where they were in this area. We hoped that by knowing what was happening, we could play some games of our own, games that would disrupt their progress. But this required people who knew something about modern science. We decided to try to devise a policy that we thought would be satisfactory.

The Cold War was as cold as war gets and the hot war was getting hotter every day. Viet Nam was boiling over and Americans were taking to the streets in protest. Abbie Hoffman had threatened to put LSD into the Chicago drinking water and our Oxford group had just determined that the Soviets were going to transfer biological weapons to the Vietnamese.

British intelligence had received information about a new bacterial strain developed by the Soviets. It was a subspecie of the common intestinal bacterium, *E. coli*. This strain, however, was invasive and could cause serious intestinal bleeding and even death. The bacterium had been developed to have also a tremendous resistance to known antibiotics. We presumed that this was done by utilizing the process of natural selection.

Bacteria that survive progressively higher concentrations of otherwise lethal antibiotics in their growth medium are permitted to replicate. This process selects for any minor mutation that might give the bacterium a slight resistance;

that bug is allowed to replicate and any additional mutations are selected for by the same process. Over many "bug" generations, this results in resistant strains. Very laborious and tedious, and not forefront science. I always find it amusing when people deny the existence of evolutionary processes when we actually utilize them directly in producing new strains of bacteria!

What concerned us also about these bacteria was that they seemed to work slowly. Unlike *E. histolytica* infections where there are massive invasions of the intestinal wall by the amoebae, followed by hemorrhage, the transformed bacteria worked slowly, creating chronic intestinal bleeding and debilitating the victims. This was almost more disastrous for an army than killing its soldiers, since seriously ill men would have to be cared for; taken back from the front, they would fill hospitals and take medical care away from wounded men. If you simply killed the guys, they wouldn't need food or medical attention and could be stacked like cordwood until taken home. This kind of bacterial warfare would tax the medical ability of any army to sustain an effective field force. Imagine a division moving toward the front with half its men suffering diarrhea!

We first began to suspect the existence of this bacterial strain when two Soviet microbiologists became violently ill while at a scientific conference in France. They refused to accept any French medical attention and were airlifted out by a special Aeroflot plane. They died en route home. Somehow, they had become infected. We later learned that they may have come in contact with the altered bugs through defective latex gloves. Soviet hospital supplies were very poor indeed and sterility was hard to maintain.

The Oxford Club

Some time later there was another event. One of the cultural and scientific attachés assigned to the Soviet embassy in Madrid also had the same signs. He was treated by a Spanish doctor who had the foresight to culture the sick man's stool. The results were frightening and the doctor took them to the University for consultation. On the way there, he was involved in an automobile accident and died on the sidewalk. His sample, specimens, and reports disappeared.

Except for a single, small tube of specimen. The doctor had plated a small amount of stool on an agar slant and put it into his refrigerator. Maria found it there when her group got involved and she suspected the worst. That agar slant, flown to our lab in Oxford, provided us with a culture of some very strange bacteria.

We examined these bugs in great detail in our small but very well-equipped and very private laboratory. The story was unfolding slowly but with a terrifying certainty. There was indeed a strain of altered *E. coli* that could only have been formed by artificial selection and with deliberate, evil intent. Our antibiotic armamentarium was not very large in those days, but most bacteria were still sensitive to the old standby drugs such as penicillin and streptomycin. These guys weren't. Nothing we threw at them would stop their relentless divisions. Except overt poisons. A shot of sodium azide or hypochlorite would do them in, but that was no surprise. Azide would also kill a horse and the hypochlorite turn it white.

We did have a few leads, mere hints or shadows of hints, that we decided to play. There was literally nothing else and we were grasping at anything that might give us some understanding of the Soviet work that was only suspected. I know I hedge in these words, but even now the issues cannot be discussed too specifically. It was decided that I would go into the field, and for that I needed cover.

I flew back to New York and within a few weeks had assumed a new career, that of a rare book dealer. Buying and selling arcane old volumes would provide me with a good cover for whatever travels I might have to make, and could explain otherwise inexplicable inquiries that I might have to make. Assuming my new hat as an antiquarian was not really a difficult transition for me. I had, since childhood, had an interest in old books and artifacts and I had collected assiduously. The New York auction houses all knew me by name. I knew the trade language and the customs, and with my newly printed business cards and an address in the Woolworth Building, I passed. Not lightly, of course. The old-timers who had worked their way up in the trade disliked me and considered me an arrogant snot-nose.

Which, as I look back in retrospect, I was. But then again, money is money and trade is trade.

Six months of buying and selling books and maps, six months of shmoozing with the other dealers, made me known to the American trade. With that accomplished I returned to England and my contacts in Oxford.

Once a week or so I would take the train to London and visit the bookdealers, occasionally buying, sometimes selling, and mostly learning. I worked hard to build my English cover and gradually became accepted as "that rich American bookdealer." They never learned whose money it really was.

As we began to learn more about the *E. coli*, I used my bookdealer cover to travel to Paris, Rome, and throughout Germany, ostensibly buying books. It was a splendid excuse to be somewhere, especially when a fair was in progress or when an auction sale was scheduled. I had contacts in each of these cities and I learned about Soviet scientific efforts wherever I went.

We hit paydirt in Vienna. The city was, and to some extent still is, a nest of agents. I think there are a lot of reasons for this. Much of Europe has had a long and rather pleasant flirtation with socialism. Some of that socialism is not much different from communism. It has always baffled me that Hitler's socialism and Stalin's communism were so close yet so far apart. Nazis and Commies were probably closer bedfellows than either liked to admit. And Vienna had, and has still, both.

It was here, while I was looking at the library the owner of a *schloss* had reluctantly decided to sell, that I had the conversation that broke the case.

Heinz Hintern, dissolute terminus in a long line of Austrian nobility, needed money to support his stable of youngmen. There was no more in the family coffers and he had exhausted his credit when it was discovered that he had been providing false provenances for illegally exported antiquities from Turkey. Hintern had stumbled upon the perfect plan for legitimizing the hundreds of very important and valuable antiquities that were being illegally dug up in both Turkey and Sicily and sold on the art gray market each year. Without a provenance, legitimate collectors and even museums would not buy them, or perhaps pay only very little for them. Hintern discovered that using his ancestral name, he could write a provenance that was widely believed. He simply provided a sworn letter that an artifact had been in the collection of his family since 1790 or 1834 or whatever, and that item achieved instant salability.

All this ended when, instead of providing a provenance for an illegally dug artifact, he unwittingly did so for a stolen item. Hintern narrowly missed jail time, and his only source of income evaporated.

He still had the library, however, and now was selling it. Word was leaked to a few private individuals that the books were available. Hintern did not want to sell the entire library all at one time and did not want the publicity that a major auction house sale would bring him. He had had enough of publicity.

The *schloss'* magnificent collection of color-plate books had already been parceled out to the baron of bookbreakers, Ignacio Sanscouvert. Sanscouvert had made a substantial fortune by buying plate books and atlases and dismembering them. He found a ready market for the individual maps and colored plates and was already scurrying about selling the individual plates from the Hintern library to printsellers and picture framers. Sanscouvert owed his fortune to the razor blade, but what will history say of the man who singlehandedly slashed apart thousands of books?

After selling off the plate books to Sanscouvert, Hintern contacted the Spanish book-collecting ascetic, Alfonso Cubierto, and began selling him other bits and pieces. Cubierto told Maria who told me, and I was now in Vienna looking at the Hintern collection.

In addition to books, Hintern still had a small collection of looted ancient artifacts. I stared in wonder at some of the delicate and brilliant Etruscan gold jewelry and the plump little Venus figurines he had displayed in a glass cabinet. "These are going to Viet Nam," boasted Hintern. "By diplomatic pouch." Hintern seemed to trust me. He liked to correct my German accent, which made him sound very important.

I tried to look bored. "Vietnamese collecting this stuff?"

"No and yes." Hintern seemed at first reluctant to discuss it, but evidently Maria had planted the right kind of information and he seemed to want to trust me on this matter also. Probably hoped to get a better price from me. "No. Soviets. They have some deal going with some North Vietnamese bigshots and want to try out some new weapon. The Viet Cong don't like it but they have one of their generals on the take. He collects ancient artifacts. The Soviets figure that these will clinch the deal." It was truly remarkable how much information someone with Hintern's positions could acquire.

Hintern needed money. I had money. And Hintern knew that if he dealt with the Soviets on this one he would owe them big. Me, he would owe nothing. We struck a deal and I paid for the artifacts with cash. I passed on the books.

It was a simple matter to pack the artifacts in my checked baggage and fly to London. With nothing to declare, I walked briskly through customs and caught the train to Oxford.

"It's too much of a long shot, Manasek." Lo Ban and the others were unconvinced. But it was the only possibility we had. There were no other leads in this miserable situation. Now we had the possibility that a North Vietnamese general was willing to field test a Soviet secret weapon in exchange for some antiquities. And we had those antiquities. And we thought we knew what the weapon was.

Suddenly things began to happen.

We learned, early one morning, that Hintern was dead. He had been found floating in the ice-choked Danube. He had been tortured horribly and was dead before he hit the river. His torture had been professionally applied and clearly designed to elicit information. It was not some boyish indiscretion. At that point we knew we were on the right trail.

Later that same day I received a cable from my New York office. A Thai businessman had contacted me about buying the Hintern trove. It wasn't clear how he had learned I had it, but we surmised that that information was among the last that Hintern ever gave anyone.

Lo Ban recognized the businessman's name. Apparently this Thai was involved in a brisk trade with both North and South Vietnam. But the North part of his trading triangle had never been proved. The guy was good at concealment and covered his trail well. But Lo Ban was convinced that he was feeding both sides and that his interest in the Hintern trove wasn't accidental. Recovering this stuff would put him in good standing with a major military officer in the North. He might not even know about the secret weapon, he might just be in it for the immediate money.

We didn't care. We were going to use this guy to get at the secret weapon and those who planned to use it. For this job, we had our own secret weapon. Lo Ban. This was his turf and he was going in to do his stuff.

We hoped we would be able to get to the Thai businessman and get him to lead us to the biological weapons. If they existed at all, that is. It would mean that Lo Ban would go undercover and attempt to penetrate the Thai/Viet group. Lo Ban helped us develop a plan and his expertise with the region and its languages was of great value.

Ultimately, the plan was a simple one. I would go to Thailand with the artifacts, sell them to the Thai broker and then Lo Ban would take over. What "take over" really meant was not spelled out. I don't think any of us really wanted to know.

The Bamboo Bar in the Oriental Hotel in Bangkok was something out of a movie set. Rattan, palms, overhead fans, hushed conferences. The works. I got there early for my appointment with the Thai, whose name was Pen Thok. But Pen Thok was even earlier. We joked a bit about our obsessively punctual behavior and I immediately liked the guy.

"It is great that you were coming here anyway," said Thok. "What are the manuscripts you buy here?"

My cover as a rare book dealer had come in handy. After getting his cable, I had told Thok that I was on my way to Bangkok to look at some manuscripts and could meet him to discuss the ancient artifacts I had obtained from Hintern. "Horoscopes," I replied to Thok. "Horoscopes that have these wonderful little drawings and divination symbols.

The ones on *Khoi* paper. Also some of the *Kammavacas* on lacquer."

Thok nodded. "They are quite cheap here. But is there a market for them in the West?"

"Not a big one, but one that's good enough if the manuscripts are nice. I have a small institutional market for the astrological ones and a decorator market for the kammavacas."

We chatted a bit. Clearly Thok was checking out my bona-fides. Then the talk turned to the artifacts and Hintern. Thok was a good poker player. I told him that I had heard that Hintern was dead and wondered what happened. Thok looked surprised and avowed that he hadn't known of Hintern's death. I almost believed him.

Talk turned to money, and, could Thok see the artifacts?

No, they were in Hong Kong with my associate who was trying to sell them to "some military guy." But I doubted the sale would go through and I was certain that we would have the artifacts in Bangkok in a day or so.

Thok showed a brief flicker of anger at the mention of a military interest in the artifacts. Was he being edged out of a deal? Whether he believed me or not, the seed of doubt had been planted.

I telephoned Lo Ban from my hotel room, making no effort to check the line for taps. I just assumed it had them. Lo Ban always stayed at the Aster Hotel in Kowloon. He knew the owners and preferred it to the better hotels on the island. We played the conversation straight. I explained to him that Thok was serious about the buy and that if his "military man" was the least bit hesitant we wanted the artifacts here the next day. "Lo Ban," I said, "our firm wants to make money and I don't care where we sell them, as long as we sell them. I think Thok's a straight shooter and I think we can close the deal in a hurry and get back home. So if your guy doesn't buy them today, bring them here and let's sell them to Thok."

Two days later Lo Ban arrived in Bangkok with our artifacts and an invented story about "missing the sale with that military guy." We met with Thok in my hotel room, Lo Ban sitting behind me while Thok examined the artifacts. It was obvious that he really didn't know too much about them; they could have been made yesterday for all he knew. "I am buying these for a colleague," Thok announced, "and I would like to have him see them before we pay you."

"No problem." I tried to be as nonchalant as possible. We still had no idea who the buyer actually was and if there was any connection to the Vietcong or to the field test of lethal bacteria. We agreed to meet in Thok's office the next day where, he assured us, the deal would take place.

I assumed that that meant his buyer would be there, the mysterious general. But I didn't ask. "I finished buying the manuscripts I wanted," I told Thok, "and I want to leave Bangkok tomorrow. If you want the artifacts, then we'll have to do the deal before tomorrow afternoon. And I'll need the money by then, too. We're on the 6 o'clock flight to Singapore." Thok agreed. I would be paid on the spot.

The three of us went and had a drink together at Thok's club. I had the feeling that Lo Ban and I were being scrutinized, perhaps looked over to see if anyone could recognize us. I am sure Thok was not entirely certain that we were who we said we were. Thok looked tired and somewhat worried. He didn't really understand this business with the artifacts, he had no appreciation for antiquity. But he knew money and power and he knew that if he could pull off this deal his ties to the Vietcong general would be assured. And there would be a fortune in it for him at the end of the road. He was clearly an ostentatious spender — he liked his jewelry big and flashy. Nonetheless, he had a great personal charm, a charisma and genuine likability. I found myself wishing I could know him better. I wanted to trust him, even though I knew what he was doing in the war and what had happened to Hintern. He probably was involved with that one, and given the need, would probably do the same to me.

Lo Ban and I kept our cover; we were running at maximum paranoia. We had a few drinks at the Bamboo Bar and we were careful to keep our conversation completely safe — we discussed only the manuscripts, the artifacts, profit and loss, and the usual business talk of antiquaries. Let them eavesdrop!

As usual, we were early for our appointment with Thok, but he was ready for us. And so was the mysterious collector for whom Thok was pimping. Lo Ban and I both immediately recognized the man sitting in Thok's office. We had studied pictures of all the North Vietnamese generals and this guy was a biggie. I hoped that Lo Ban and I could keep our poker faces. It would not do to recognize him if we wanted to walk out of that building. General_____ didn't say much. He looked at the Hintern trove and the god of Greed took over. Lo Ban excused himself as the General fondled the artifacts. He returned just as the General made a slight gesture with his hand.

Thok took Lo Ban and me aside. "It's all here," he said as he handed me the attaché case filled with US hundreds. "Thank you very much." Thok dismissed us.

"Quickly, Manasek!" Lo Ban hissed a warning as we walked briskly down the street outside Thok's office. We bumped into a Chinese woman and Lo Ban apologized profusely. I recall that she was particularly beautiful, but took no further notice. For at that instant there was the roar of an explosion as the second floor of Thok's office building was blown outward, showering us all with glass and shards.

"Quickly, Manasek!" Lo Ban pushed me into a taxicab and he spoke quickly to the driver in fluent Thai. The cab took off in a belch of exhaust and we hurtled to the airport, leaving behind a fetid vapor trail of diesel exhaust.

"Lo Ban! The suitcase — that attaché case — the money!" I suddenly discovered that the money was missing. Lo Ban signaled me to be quiet and I acquiesced, not really understanding, but assuming that all was under control. We did not speak during the quick ride to the airport, nor did I question him when the lovely Chinese woman, the same one into whom we had crashed just a bit earlier, gave us each a worn but expensive attache case as carry-on. "Your cover," she said. "You can't get on a flight with absolutely nothing!"

"Thank you, Amanda." Lo Ban gave her a quick hug and added, "See you in Hong Kong."

Two days later we were sitting in the Peninsula having drinks. I had slept poorly and was still trying to understand the events of the past few days. After the explosion in Bangkok, we had gotten on a flight to Hong Kong. When we landed in Hong Kong we learned that the shuttle flight from Bangkok to Singapore, the one we told Thok we were taking, crashed with all on board killed. And here we were, in Hong Kong but without the money for the artifacts. And Thok and the general and the artifacts probably blown to shreds.

I was on my second martini when Lo Ban's Chinese friend came in. She was even more beautiful than I remembered from Bangkok. Amanda had brought with her two small cases. The first had our money and the second had the Hintern trove.

"Amanda knows a lot of people in the antiquities trade here in Hong Kong," said Lo Ban as explanation. "This stuff was easy to copy."

I never asked Lo Ban about the explosion. And he never explained it. For all I know it was a coincidental accident.

The bacteria were never used in Vietnam. I live still with the ambiguity of not knowing if anything we did prevented the use of the bugs, or if all we accomplished was to kill a few people and have an airplane of innocents blown up.

The Corner Piece[1]

> When a man is in a house and opens his eyes he will first notice
> the interior of the room and only later will he see the view
> outside the windows.
>
> — *The Teaching of Buddha*

About 70 rare book and map dealers from all over the world,
including myself, were exhibiting at the International Book
Fair. We were displaying rare and ancient volumes, not so
ancient first editions, some medieval manuscripts, and a
smattering of prints and maps. In addition there were the
dealers who specialized in secondhand books, the type you
might find in your local used bookshop.

Gobs of money change hands at shows like this one.
The dealer whose booth was next to mine sold over $90,000
worth of rare books to other dealers before the fair was
even open to the public. My specialty is rare maps. I wasn't
so lucky. The only pre-fair business I had was from the
weird guy who sneaked in, past security, to sell me a roll of
old maps. He knew what he had and didn't give me a really
good deal, just sort of an OK price. Most of the maps were
originals, but a couple of them were fakes, probably from
the Continent, as is common these days. One of the fakes
had a chunk torn out of it. No big deal. It was garbage
anyway.

1. This work was published in substantially the same form under the title: *Opening
Night at the Book Fair* in: AB Bookman's Weekly, March 27, 1995. © 1995 F.J.
Manasek. All rights reserved.

While pre-opening business was slow for me, opening night itself was turning out OK and I took advantage of a lull to get a martini. I was walking slowly, returning from the bar with my drink, trying to navigate the carpeted aisle thick with clusters of people standing around talking. Dealers telling lies about the ones that got away and telling lies about the ones that didn't. Dealers trying to impress buyers, buyers trying to browbeat dealers. A few people looked dazed, as though they didn't know why they were even at such a demented activity. Others, like I, were trying not to spill their overpriced drinks.

The aisle ran to my exhibit booth from the side of the exhibition hall where the bar was set up. It went past several other booths, some of which were filled with eager buyers. Even at the booths with no customers, the resident dealers were trying to look as though they had just made a great sale. No downcast faces here. Further down the aisle was a small curtained-off corner area filled with packing boxes and bookcases.

I glanced idly at the blue curtain surrounding the corner storage area. It wasn't quite long enough to reach the floor. There was a gap between it and the red carpet. The gap was just big enough to let me notice a leg. A woman's leg.

Ever discreet, I kept going. Back to my booth. Were the rumors about Lo Ban possibly true? I had known him for years and found the rumors very unlikely.

Lo Ban was a dealer who dealt in illustrated books, primarily the Japanese and Chinese ones printed with woodblocks. He also enjoyed the company of women and, in his younger days, sometimes traveled with a large bevy of "assistants." Rumors about Lo Ban abounded. Some claimed to have seen him in indiscreet situations during book fairs. It was even rumored that Lo Ban and one of his companions had amused themselves during a lull in a

Sotheby's sale in London the previous autumn. But those of us who knew Lo Ban well knew that many of these rumors were untrue and were just the vicious vicarious confabulations of the jealous, the have-nots and can't-do's.

I shrugged and put Lo Ban out of my mind while taking care of a couple of customers who were interested in the set of Blaeu maps I had on display. Beautiful hand colored maps, from the 1650s, showing the world and each of the continents. My customers examined each square inch of all five maps with a magnifying glass. Then they examined the backs. We discussed price, condition, price, color, and price. Finally I was able to close the deal at a bit under twenty thousand dollars. I walked over to the wrapping desk with my clients and their maps. I took a quick peek under the blue curtain as I walked by. The space was still there. The leg was still there. In the same position.

After seeing my clients to the door with their wrapped set of maps, I hurried back to the curtained area. The crowd had picked up a bit and several groups of people were standing around the area when I got back. I edged through them, pulled the curtain back a bit, and looked in.

I know a stiff when I see one, and this was one. Her neck and face were all purple and large amounts of frothy saliva had run from her open mouth. There was a bright yellow electrical extension cord wrapped around her neck. She had apparently been deposited on a stack of empty boxes, and from the appearance of her dress, she had slipped down from them, almost spilling out into the aisle. Had she not slipped down she would probably not have been noticed for another two days when, at the end of the fair, dealers would come looking for their packing boxes.

She still wore an exhibitor's badge. I peered down to read it. Cornella Sims. I recognized neither her nor her name. She was not a dealer and I hadn't seen her assisting at anyone's booth. Possibly someone's helper, but not one I'd seen at this fair.

I pulled the curtain closed and backed away.

Peter Miles, smiling over a martini, came over to me. "What the hell's the matter with you?"

"Just found a body, Peter, nothing else."

"Ha, Ha!" Peter appreciated a good joke and tried to make me think this was one of them. "Ha, ha! Very good." He edged away, smiling and nodding his head as if in appreciation. "Have a good fair." Peter was one of the most aggressive map dealers exhibiting at the fair. Years ago he had dealt only in 19th-century American atlas maps. The sorts of things one ripped out of Mitchell and Johnson atlases. Thirty-dollar items. Now, he dealt in five figure maps. He had secured a big chunk of capital somewhere and nobody knew how.

Except me. I knew that Peter had been introduced to an elderly lady who was selling off her late husband's collections, and he had bought several atlases. She had, unknowingly, sold him some gems, the least of which was a splendid, complete deJode atlas in original full color. I think Peter had paid her $2000. for the book. I discovered this much later when she was selling me some other items. I had found her husband's handwritten inventory and asked what had happened to the atlases.

"Ha, ha!" Peter still chortled.

Peter aside, I still had to deal with this body. One of the rent-a-cops came down the aisle. Book fair security. Easy duty for them. Despite the millions worth of rare items on display, there was very little theft and never any disorder at rare book fairs. I went up to the rent-a-cop and got his attention. "There's a real problem here. Please get the promoter over here right away. Tell him its an emergency."

"What is the nature of the problem? Has anything been perpetrated?" The rent-a-cop was talking cop talk. This could take years.

"Look, asshole, there's a dead body here. Go fetch the promoter."

The rent-a-cop looked at me. I looked at him. "I'll be in my booth," I said, "number 122."

I was bigger than he was and he decided not to press the issue. About half an hour later he returned to my booth with the promoter, Xavier Saperstein, who was, as usual, scratching his itch.

"All right, what the hell's going on here?"

I looked up from my *London Times* crossword puzzle. "Saperstein, I don't get this. 'East Anglian beauty queen's dog. Midnight.' And it's only four letters. You got a stiff in the alley behind booth 233."

"Manasek, you're a goddamn troublemaker. You're a fucking menace. This is the last show you're doing with me." Saperstein the promoter was pissed. Saperstein had hemorrhoids and a personality to match. He walked away, scratching.

"Yo, Saperstein, Booth 233's the other direction."

"Manasek, you're a goddamn troublemaker and this is the last show you're doing with me."

The mother of all screams pierced the air. It cut through like a scimitar. Then another scream. And another. Nothing in the world sounded like a bunch of New York broads screaming holy murder. A flock of ululating Palestinian women would be no match.

"Saperstein, you got a stiff in the alley behind booth 233. And, what's four letters and 'East Anglian beauty queen's dog. Midnight.'"?

Saperstein and the rent-a-cop ran to the source of the screams.

The body now was in the middle of the aisle, empty cartons tumbled about in random disorder. Freddie Spangle, the dealer in Modern Firsts was writing up a sale. Freddie hated Lo Ban, who used to touch his Modern Firsts and get fingerprints all over the DJ's. It made Freddie wince. The fellow was a bounder, obviously.

"Lo Ban! The dirty rat! He's killed her!" Freddie was screaming, too.

Meanwhile, the screamers had calmed themselves. They were having mai-tais and banana cordials at the bar. Courtesy of Saperstein. "Fix these ladies up with whatever they want," he said as he dug at the source of his annoyance, "I'll pay."

Two of the city cops who were called in began to interview nearby dealers. Saperstein, acting on another of his dislikes, had fingered Lo Ban, who was nowhere to be seen.

"He did it," said Saperstein with a degree of authority that was accentuated by keeping both hands visible.

Sanscouvert, the French bookbreaker and dealer in prints, spoke up to the cops. "Lo Ban is a nice man. He would never hurt anyone."

The New York cops were great. They got the body out of there with hardly an interruption to the book fair. But they couldn't find Lo Ban. Lo Ban was off on another adventure, helping his old friend Tony Raimo.

Tony was frightened. Frightened because some of the children's book dealers had threatened to kill him. Frightened enough that he had registered at the hotel under an assumed name. Tony, it seems, had bought an unopened publisher's case of *Peter Rabbit* firsts at a Salvation

36

Army shop and was planning to retire on the proceeds. The Children's Book Establishment didn't like that, and Tony was no fool. He hid his *Peter Rabbit* in a girl friend's place in Bayonne.

The cops were methodically interviewing all the dealers, some of whom didn't like the interruption of business. "Hey, do I come into the station house and talk to you when you're working?"

"You discovered the deceased?" The cop now came to me.

"Yes, Officer, I did."

We got all the details about how and times and that kind of stuff done. Then we got down to business.

"Got any ideas who done it?" Now a Suit was talking with me. He came into my booth and waved the Uniform out. "Does this mean anything to you?" He showed me a scrap of paper.

It was a torn corner of an old map. This was part of a fake, an outright forgery. The color was garish. It clearly was a Continental forgery. Recent, too.

"Where did this come from?"

"It was in her hand," said the Detective. "I think it might be a clue."

I drew myself up in faux indignation. "It is not a map that anyone here would have been selling. Why, it's clearly a forgery. I am shocked to the very bone. The very thought that someone exhibiting at this fair would even have such a map is beyond belief. I suspect it was an outsider. Nobody here would even have such a map." I said that with conviction. "Perhaps, though, you might search the map dealers here and see if anyone has a similar map. Start with me."

"Oh, ha — well, I'll be back, certainly." He was obviously embarrassed at the suggestion that he search my inventory first and he went off to find the other map dealers.

I picked through the roll of maps I had bought before the fair opened and pulled out the fake. The one with the missing corner. I made sure that Peter was away from his booth when I came over to visit, map in hand. He was off shmoozing, trying to buy an Ortelius atlas from one of the German dealers. I leafed idly through the pile of maps on his table. Just the place for it, I thought, as I left him a present, slipping it in amongst the larger maps. They'll be bound to discover the missing piece.

The Deaccessioning
of Reiji Sato

Things do not come and do not go, neither do they appear nor disappear; therefore, one does not get things or lose things.
— *The Teaching of Buddha*

Somebody had told Reiji Sato that I was a dealer in Japanese prints and books.

That was only partly true. I used to be quite active in that area and, for a time, traveled regularly between Japan and the US, bringing back suitcases packed with those wonderful old woodblock printed books, the *ehon*. If I filled up a suitcase with Western books I couldn't lift it, but the Japanese books were light. Delicate looking things, many were not collected very seriously in Japan and the country seemed knee-deep in them. I recall a shop in Kyoto literally filled with stacks of woodblock books; they had boxes full piled outside, shielded from the elements by only an awning. And cheap, even by the standards of those days. Half the contents of that store ultimately found its way to this country, via my suitcases. Now those same books are no longer Japan's throwaways. They are sold individually, not by the suitcaseful. Unfortunately, I am no longer a force in this area and I no longer travel back from Japan with cases of books. My inventory is now very different.

Reiji came into my Hanover office unannounced one afternoon and we began a long, careful conversation; the first of many.

"Watakushi ni namae wa Manasek des. Dozo yo roshiko." I smiled at him and motioned him to a seat.

Reiji smiled back. He hadn't expected me to speak Japanese. We exchanged cards and began the first of our long interactions, interactions which appeared to be mostly quiet periods punctuated by a few words, then more silence. Reiji seemed a man trapped between cultures; a man trying to adapt to the American way. He obviously had been schooled in American behavior before his company, Dai-ichi Harawata, sent him over for his two year American stint, and he was applying his lessons. The casualness he affected sat rather well with him; he clearly liked the American informality and unstructured ways.

I had very little to offer him since my stock of Japanese books was low. But he did buy, much to his delight, a brilliant set of *Ehon koji-dan* complete in 13 volumes. And a Meiji imprint of Hokusai's *Hyaku fuku*.

Reiji Sato, who had grown up in Chiba, a little city now part of the Tokyo sprawl, was surprised to learn that I, too, had lived in Chiba for a while some years ago. We reminisced briefly, and it turned out that neither of us had particularly liked Chiba.

I recalled that in those days I couldn't wait until I had time off so I could catch the train to Tokyo and spend a free evening or weekend with Nikki, who had a splendid flat in Akasaka. Both Reiji and I grew wistful as we remembered our younger days. Such wistfulness increased when we would share a bottle of Suntory scotch. Halfway through one of these, he confessed to feeling trapped and powerless. He longed after the sort of freedom I had.

A graduate of the elite Tokyo University, Reiji was destined for rapid advancement in the Dai-ichi Harawata ranks. Like so many Japanese, he had grown up more or less unaware of the wonderful artifacts of his own culture and discovered them, quite by accident, in American museums. He became a regular visitor at the Boston Museum of Fine Arts, where one of the world's great Japanese art collections resides. And he bought voraciously, but with a sophistication that few beginning collectors had.

Reiji came to Hanover many times in the next year and we became friends. He worked in the New York offices of his firm and he and his wife lived in the Little Japan that had sprouted in Scarsdale. Keiko, his wife, spoke fluent English; better than her husband's. She, however, hated America.

"Women have all the power in Japan," Reiji laughed. "They control the home and whoever controls that controls everything."

Keiko glared at him.

"In America, women share power. They get to run business but they give up real power to do that. Keiko doesn't like that." Reiji had a twinkle in his eye when he said that, but Keiko glowered.

"He thinks he is American," scoffed Keiko. "He doesn't even use chopstick anymore. Big house in Scarsdale and backyard barbecue. And he spends all his money on his books." The "instead of me" was implicit. Keiko had a bad case of the vanities.

I saw little of Reiji in the next few months. He was going back home and was busy with those arrangements. Japanese firms don't like to have their executives spend too much time abroad. I thought little about him or his collection until I was at the Chicago Book Fair and spent some time in idle gossip.

I was talking with Lo Ban about Reiji and his collection. Lo Ban had the adjacent booth at the fair and had let it slip that he was going to take care of shipping the collection. "He's got a great collection." Lo Ban leaned back in his chair. "I think he skimmed the cream of whatever was on the American market in the past year or so."

"Except for that Maxwell Parrish print he bought at a local auction. He likes it, but it doesn't fit into his collection. And now it goes back home. Do a good job packing it." I sipped my martini. The show was deadly. Chicago was grey and cold. And the restaurants mediocre. I felt sorry for myself for being here.

"Chicago is supposed to have great little ethnic restaurants and every one I've tried is dreadful."

Lo Ban laughed. "Trouble with you, Manasek, is that you are gullible. You actually believe people. Me, I know about ethnics. If that food is so goddamn good, why aren't the restaurants bigger? Why aren't people waiting in lines to get in?"

Lo Ban's logic often eluded me and I was glad I didn't have to pursue the subject with him. Someone had entered his booth and he was, for the moment, busy. He was smiling when he came back a few minutes later, but it was a paper smile. "I hate this goddamn city," said Lo Ban still smiling.

The Chicago show dragged on and on. Lo Ban and I ran out of things to talk about. By unspoken mutual agreement, we never discussed the Old Days, those days when he and I and our friends were in Asia.

I asked again about the Sato collection. "Is it going by air or sea? Why hadn't Reiji let his company ship it for him?" Whenever I brought up the subject of the Sato collection, Lo Ban tried to change the topic. Hard to do when there was nothing else to talk about. But he clearly did not want to discuss the Sato collection.

The book fair boredom got worse, festering like some carbuncle twixt the buttocks of the mind. Even Amanda had jumped ship. "This place gives me the creeps. I'm outta here!"

"Where are you off to?" asked Lo Ban.

"Hong Kong."

"She might well be," smiled Lo Ban as he stretched out his legs and sighed.

"Cut the crap, Lo Ban. What's with the Sato collection?" I wasn't about to let the topic die, but Lo Ban just got up and waited on an imaginary customer.

Two days after the Chicago Fair, they found Reiji's car. It was parked near the Tappan Zee Bridge. The note they found on the driver's seat said simply, "I do not go back." There was a neat pile of wallet, eyeglasses, and wristwatch on the bridge. The police said that suicides often do that — they can't bear to get these things wet and ruined.

Keiko went back to Japan, happier than I'd ever seen her. They never found Reiji's body and I heard some rumblings about how Reiji's collection somehow got lost en route to Japan. Must have pleased Keiko.

Lo Ban wouldn't return my calls. Since Amanda had indeed gone to Hong Kong, perhaps Lo Ban had gone over to be with her. There was no reason to believe he was deliberately avoiding me.

There was little point in rehashing Reiji's suicide and the thought that perhaps Lo Ban knew something about it did not occur to me. Back in Vermont, I was getting somewhat bored and feeling restless. The ennui of peace. And that is always reason enough to go somewhere and to spend some time doing a little map hunting. Also, it seemed time for some rich, Bavarian food. The food at the Norwich Inn was very good, but even they couldn't do what the Bavarians could.

I rang up Annalise, a friend from our group's old days. Annalise lived near Munich. A quiet life; her neighbors never knew her history. She, predictably, was bored also and readily agreed to my suggestion that we spend some time playing together in the Black Forest.

I was off to Munich the next day.

The trip was a good one. Good food and a chance to catch up with friends and gossip. All with Annalise's wonderful company. And, moreover, I found some interesting maps in, of all places, a touristy antiques shop. The place was one of those that had musical beer steins, wallets that looked like lederhosen, and quaint carved breadboards as well as a variety of little antiques selected only because they could fit into tourist luggage.

44

Nonetheless, the shop had an Arrowsmith folding America map, a Speed Virginia and, most amazing, a deJode America. Not to arouse suspicions, I also bought the heavily foxed deVaugondy Latvia they had in with the pile. And the shopkeeper was convinced that he swindled me. Later, I pencilled a price of DM8200 in the lower right corner of the Latvia map and left it, rolled up, hidden on top of the armoire in our hotel room when we left. Whoever found it would be in for some fun!

Faithful Fiona, my part-time office helper, had handled the Hanover office affairs well during my absence. When I returned home I found bills paid, inquiries answered, my mail opened, answered and sorted. Except for one letter. It bore no return address and was carefully marked "personal and private."

It contained a single Polaroid photograph, showing the interior of a large, well-appointed room. On the table in front of a large bookcase stood a bottle of Johnny Walker Black, a propped-up *New York Times,* and several rows of upright Japanese books. I recognized my *Ehon koji-dan* and several others that I had sold to Reiji. I also recognized the Maxfield Parrish print, still looking out of place. The envelope bore a New York airport postmark. It was about as anonymous as possible, yet it told me everything. I was glad my friend Reiji let me know he was alive and happy.

Dozo, odaiji ni, watashi no tomodachi!

The Great Ohio Book Fair

Señor, señor, do you know where we're headin'?
Lincoln County Road or Armageddon?
— *Bob Dylan*

Lo Ban laid low. For the time being, at least. Ever since that dreadful incident at the International Book Fair where one of his associates was murdered, Lo Ban tried to keep a low profile. He had nothing to do with the murder and was completely exonerated by the Grand Jury that took his testimony in great detail, even though he knew nothing of interest to them with respect to the murder. Although the Grand Jury did nothing, now Lo Ban was facing a different problem. Book fair promoters and organizers didn't want him in their fairs. They never said it, but it just seemed to work out that his contracts got misplaced, his checks lost, or his booth location so bad that he didn't bother to even show up to do the fair.

"Sorry, Lo Ban, but you know that booths are assigned by impartial lottery. You got the single booth behind the men's room again. It's a very fair system, Lo Ban."

As a dealer in oriental books, mostly Chinese and
Japanese woodblock printed books, Lo Ban was facing a
supply crisis. The Chinese weren't letting older books out
of their country — the great Cultural Revolution had
destroyed so many of them that what was left was being
kept at home. His Japanese contacts were not coming
through with many of the better items and Lo Ban's
inventory was running low, particularly of the Japanese
shunga, those sexually explicit illustrated works sometimes
known as pillow books, or marital instructions. Some of
them were masterpieces, done by great woodblock artists
such as the Kambun Master, as well as the more common
works by Haronobu and Utamaro. Lo Ban was particularly
fond of the very early *tanroku-bon* books and often had, in
his inventory, splendid *tan-e* prints, the most prized *shunga*.

These great works of Japanese erotica fetched large
sums and Lo Ban had a reputation as someone who
generally had a decent supply of them for sale. He often
was able to buy these books in the United States. Some
years ago, Lo Ban had made a remarkable discovery.
American occupation forces in Japan after WWII took home
large numbers of *shunga*. Now, as the veterans were aging
and dying, their picture books were coming on the market.
Many of these soldiers had had no idea of the tradition of
Japanese *ehon*, or woodblock book, or indeed any
knowledge of Japanese erotica, but merely took these books
as examples of "dirty pictures." They would occasionally
take them down to the VFW or American Legion Post or
the B.P.O.E. Lodge and, over their Coors or Iron City brews,
giggle and snort and boast. Now these gallant warriors were
leaving this life and also wives who wanted no part of these
obscene things. Lo Ban discovered that if he set up at little

local bookfairs in the Midwest, nice *shunga* occasionally rose up from the cornfields.

It worked like this. Lo Ban spread out about a dozen soft floppy woodblock printed books that were entirely calligraphy. The locals, coming to the fair and expecting, as they often said, "normal" books, would be surprised at seeing these things.

"What kind of writing is this?" "Where do you get these?"

Of course, nobody ever bought any of the books that Lo Ban displayed. Rather, the books were his bait. Boring, tattered, shabby little things, he generally priced them very low. When asked, he emphasized that they were very important works, very rare, very old. And yet had a low price. Whenever someone commented on them, Lo Ban would say "I buy this type of book. I pay good prices."

Every once in a while it worked.

Lo Ban was in a suburb of Toledo, Ohio, exhibiting at *The Second Maumee Golden Mile Mall Rare Book and Magazine Show.* He was chumming the waters, hoping to lure some orientalia out of the flat, generic landscape. Still on his best behavior, and being a great cultural relativist, he did not bring his usual bevy of female assistants to the show. They were happily ensconced at the Maumee Tip-Top Motel, watching Chinese flicks on the cable. One of his younger assistants, Amy Yee, was busy cataloguing some Chinese manuscripts. Most people didn't realize that Amy was the brain behind Lo Ban's manuscript business and also had a big financial stake in the business.

Lo Ban had spread his books out and now waited with the patience of a true fisherman. He had endured the long day of stares, no sales, and not a single fair visitor who knew what his stuff was. Then he got a strike. The reel screamed as the line unwound, smoking through the guides. It was a real one. A Biggie.

She was wandering through the fair, a plastic shopping bag clutched to her ample bosom, eating buttered popcorn from a bright red box. Her jacket matched her shorts. A real K-Mart gal. Smart Shopper. She now lightly browsed Lo Ban's books. More than casual, idle looking, thought Lo Ban. "Very old Chinese books," said Lo Ban. "I buy them, too."

"You do? My husband brought some back from Japan. Or was it China? After the war, you know. Oh, I'm sorry..." The local Polyester had suddenly noticed Lo Ban's oriental features. "I'm sorry. I didn't mean... The war, you know..."

"It's OK." Lo Ban was gracious. "I'm American," he lied. "No problem."

"Yours don't have pictures," she said as she flipped backwards through the books. "I think my late husband's books had pictures." She blushed as she said this. Lo Ban had seen it all before.

"Sometimes," he said, "the pictures are a bit, well, *different*... I buy even those. I have foreign markets, you know."

"Oh yes, you people don't believe in God. I understand.... Oh! I'm so sorry! You just said you're American. Of course you believe in God. I'm sorry."

"Not at all, madam, I know exactly what you mean."

Polite chitchat, smiles, an exchange of the verbiage that says "I'm one of you and we're both OK," and she agreed to bring over the books for Lo Ban to look at.

She returned a few hours later with a large, soiled paper bag that contained a shoebox. The box was filled with Japanese printed *shunga.*

"I can show these to *you,*" she said. "I could never show them to people. My husband was in the Air Force and brought these back. He never really looked at them. He wasn't that kind of person."

"Of course not," Lo Ban purred his mild purr and smiled as engagingly as he could.

There were about two dozen softcover, sewn Japanese books in the box. All were in pretty good condition. Lo Ban recognized several at once. There were a number of books by Kinobu, and an album by Settei. These he instantly recognized. There was a beautiful two volume copy of *Makura-byobu,* a *sumizuri-e* book done in the late 1660s by the brilliant Kambun Master; truly a museum piece. A few were trivial, late-19th-century wank books. The kind that were cranked out by the hundreds and that showed no artistic merit. Decorticate genitalia.

Lo Ban lowballed the lot. The owner balked at Lo Ban's bid. Employing every bit of his vast psychological cunning, Lo Ban began to spread out the opened books, displaying their contents to the passersby, who seemed to be drawn to them by some mysterious force. It was a gesture designed to unnerve the seller. And it did. She kept closing the books and Lo Ban kept opening them. Finally he added a bit to the offer and, just to get away from that awful scene, before her neighbors might see her near this stuff, the seller accepted his offer. A wad of hundred dollar bills changed hands and Lo Ban put the pile of books under the table.

He smiled graciously at the woman. "A very good price, I assure you." For whom, he did not specify.

Lo Ban deadpanned. He did not change expression, not wanting to portray even a hint of gloating. He had learned early in his career not to reveal post-deal emotions. Without looking around he moved his foot into contact with the box under the table. A comforting contact. Lo Ban would clear thousands on this one. He was not the least ashamed by the low price he paid for the books. This was a two-way street. Had he not been here, investing his time and money and knowledge in setting up at the *The Second Maumee Golden Mile Mall Rare Book and Magazine Show*, she would not have known what to do with her late husband's books. To her they were just dirty pictures and she was ashamed of them. She probably would not have even gotten them appraised — she wasn't the sort of person who could admit that her husband had these things. The dumpster or the fire were the most likely possibilities. Now they were safe. And Lo Ban's trip into the Great American Heartland had been worthwhile.

He lapsed into thought. Very pleasant thought, indeed. About Amanda Chin, his long-time companion on these trips. Lo Ban was lost in fantasy and did not notice the two little children who were playing by the edge of his table. Their mother was looking at the back issues of *TV Guide* that were for sale at the adjacent booth. She was engrossed in a couple of Rock Hudson issues.

"Real scarce items," assured the dealer. "These are getting very hard to find in this nice condition."

Suddenly she shrieked. "My God!" Instantly Lo Ban returned to reality. Fantasy over, the real world needed him.

Lo Ban looked down. The two little kids had found his box. They had opened it and were playing with his wonderful *shunga*. And their mother had seen. There was nothing that Lo Ban could do to cover up the event. He had immediate visions of getting arrested. "Chinese pornographer terrorizes mall," and similar nighttime news caps crossed his mind.

"LeRoy! LouAnn! Oh, Lord Jesus save my children!" Momma had a fit. LeRoy and LouAnn found more pictures and were busily turning pages. They were not about to listen to their mother's demands that they get up and "put them books from Satan away."

Lo Ban dived down to retrieve his books before grubby little fingers did more damage than the previous two centuries. He quickly snatched them and tucked them back into the box. "Wanna see! Wanna see!" cried little LouAnn and little LeRoy.

"Their daddy will deal with you, you disgusting person! How dare you bring them disgusting pictures (she actually said 'pitchers') where there are families."

"They are Chinese art, madam. They are not disgusting pictures." Lo Ban had found it easier, at times like this, to call the *shunga* "Chinese" rather than Japanese. For some reason it made it less threatening. "They are not for children, certainly, but you should keep your children under control, madam."

After she left, Lo Ban quickly scooped up the books he had on display and tossed them into his suitcase. The table cover went in next and he still had room for his *shunga*. He was going to split and split fast. This could be an ugly scene and, once again, Lo Ban would be in trouble. "Chinese pornographer torn to shreds by howling Maumee mob." As he left, he heard mutterings about that "Godless Communist sex prevert."

A few hours later Lo Ban thought the episode was finished. Amanda was kneading his neck and Lo Ban was sipping the Johnny Walker Black that she had poured for him. The two other, much younger, women were watching Chinese flicks on the motel cable TV. Amy was sending a fax to Hong Kong. Then they heard the knock.

The man at the door was The Reverend Jimmy-John Dean. "Call me Jimmy-John. I'm LouAnn and LeRoy's daddy," said The Reverend Dean to Lo Ban. Lo Ban kept his cool but was more than a little bit disturbed. He knew these people could be violent and probably carried guns. "Come in," said Lo Ban in a graciously disarming manner. "What can I do for you?"

"Well, it's like this," said Jimmy-John. "My kids found some of your books. You know, the ones with, er, pitchers in 'em. Can I see them?"

"I'm sorry," said Lo Ban in his professional Chinese voice with just an added trace of accent, "those books are not available. They are Chinese art books and I'm truly sorry that your children found them. They were in a box under the table and were not on display."

"Don't gimme that shit about Chinese art books. Them's Jap *shunga*. I preached in Japan. Before I founded my church, that is."

"You started a church?" Lo Ban feigned interest. "Would you like some scotch, Father?"

"Father? Shit! That's Pope-talk. I'm a real Christian, not a snapper. Don't gimme that 'father' shit. Jus' call me

Jimmy-John. Yeah, I got a church. The Maumee Miracle True Church of God. Scotch? Shit! I drink bourbon. Got any?"

"Sorry, we don't. Just scotch. Amanda will get you some, if you like."

Jimmy-John turned around and saw Amanda. "Holy shit! Where'd you get the dish?"

Now Jimmy-John was treading in Lo Ban's territory; he had crossed the line. And Lo Ban had him figured out. He stared at Jimmy-John and in an icy voice said "Just what do you want here?"

Mild, innocuous Lo Ban was suddenly dangerous and Jimmy-John realized it. Lo Ban's eyes lost their sparkle and filled with the cold cobra-look of death. As though smitten, Jimmy-John felt a chill permeate him. A wave of cold fear penetrated every atom of his body. He fought to control himself and not show it, but the fear escaped. It oozed through every pore and orifice and filled the room. Jimmy-John and Lo Ban both knew it.

Jimmy-John changed the subject. "Can I see your *shunga*. Please? I might wanna buy some." Jimmy-John giggled and put his hand in his trouser pocket.

"This is all we have available." Lo Ban handed him a single slender volume (one only of three) and said "I can sell you this one."

It wasn't very good. Content as well as condition. Smudged and printed poorly, the book had also suffered physically over the years. But it did have 'pitchers' and that's what Jimmy-John wanted. "How much?"

"Thousand" said Lo Ban, still icy-voiced and cobra-eyed.

Under Cover

"Sweet Jesus." Reverend Jimmy-John peeled ten centuries off his roll. "Why so much?"

"Quality." Lo Ban handed him the book. "Good night."

Half an hour later, Lo Ban and his friends were speeding through the dark Midwestern night, treadmilling tires moving mile after featureless mile beneath them. Lo Ban had figured out Jimmy-John and was taking no chances. He didn't want an ugly scene.

Which was just what was taking place back at the Maumee Tip-Top Motel. Just as Lo Ban had expected, The Reverend Jimmy-John decided on revenge. To even the playing field he brought three of his deacons and they all had their baseball bats. They broke into Lo Ban's motel room, and, not finding anyone there, they did the next logical thing: ransack the place. All they found were a drawer full of women's undergarments, which they threw around the room in anger. And, of course, the bottles of bourbon, which they couldn't pass up. And that's how the cops, acting on a tip, found them.

The Unpleasantness at the Amsterdam Book Fair

> If a king is plagued by bandits, he must find out where their camp is before he can attack them.
> — *The Teaching of Buddha*

I took a suitcase of atlases and maps to Amsterdam last March even though I wasn't exhibiting at the book fair.

The fair was smaller than usual; it was largely a European event. About 40 dealers were there, only two were American. Although I've never had much success selling to the Amsterdam trade, I knew the fair would be well attended by the other European trade to whom I usually sold well. Most American and English dealers shared this problem with me and many of us don't even try to sell our better things to the Dutch dealers. Nonetheless, hope springs eternal and this was spring. It was a lovely March in Amsterdam. The crocuses were out and the dafs and tulips were trying. I had left behind a particularly sticky Vermont mud season and was happy to be in the pleasant surroundings of this great city, especially appreciating the month's jump on spring.

The fair was held, as usual, in the RAI congress center, a sprawling, antiseptic convention complex some distance from the heart of Amsterdam. This meant a taxi from and a taxi back to my hotel near the Rijksmuseum. The trolleys worked well, but using them meant a longish walk and besides, I avoid public transport in general. Specifically when lugging stuff.

I did rather well on the first day of the fair, just flogging my atlases quietly and privately. I met with some European clients, and even with an English collector who had come over to see me. After opening night, traffic fell off rapidly and the floor was virtually empty the next day. I then had time to touch bases with the American dealers, Jeff Mancevice, and Lo Ban.

Jeff was not having a good fair, but he took it philosophically. He is a major American dealer. At his level of trade, one poor fair doesn't mean much. It's all advertising, anyway. Or so we tell ourselves. Lo Ban took a more personal, histrionic view of these events. He loved action for the sake of action rather than for the sake of making money. He hardly needed more. But still, Lo Ban was perplexed. Amsterdam was usually a good fair for him and he usually sold large numbers of western items as well as the oriental books that were his specialty. Europe, Amsterdam in particular, seemed to be a black hole for this type of material. But more than poor sales, something else was bothering Lo Ban.

"What's happening, Lo Ban," I asked. "Anybody after you?" It was supposed to be funny.

Amanda Chin, Lo Ban's companion, suddenly decided to go for coffee. She didn't like talk about troubles. Lo Ban fidgeted. "Manasek," he said, "They're using the trade to run drugs. I'm on to them and they're going to ice me."

"Who the hell are they? Lo Ban, what's happening! This is a book fair. What are you ranting about?" Lo Ban and I had known each other years ago in the Orient. We never talked about it and nobody else connected us with those events, but we had been through some amazing adventures together. And we could still be a team. Nobody could break that. Now, according to Lo Ban, Amsterdam drug lords had figured that rare books were an ideal way to get drugs into the US. It was unlikely that Customs would look too carefully at a load of old books coming into the country for a book fair. And because he knew it, he was in trouble and needed help.

"Remember the old days, Lo Ban," I said quietly. "Venceremos."

"Thanks, Manasek. This one's too big for me to handle alone. I'm getting too old for this sort of thing. But old man de Bruin isn't. He told me about it. That bugger's at least 90 years old. Knows a lot of people."

"And still a Nazi." I volunteered. "The OSS covered for him after the war and he was never prosecuted. He's been playing footsie with the CIA ever since. About what, I don't know." I also wondered why the old Nazi would have warned Lo Ban, but kept that worry to myself. For the time being.

Lo Ban hissed. "Manasek," he said to me quietly, "do you see that little fellow in the Armani suit over in Pieter de Hooch's booth?"

"Yes I do. But I don't know him. Why do you ask?"

"He's been in my booth several times. I don't know what he's doing, but he's messing with my books."

"You're nuts, Lo Ban." I could not understand his concern about the neurotic behavior of a book fair pest at a time like this.

"Seriously, Manasek, that guy is a friend of de Hooch's. He came into my booth and took books off the shelf, fussed with them and moved them to other shelves. Never asked about them, isn't interested in buying any, and doesn't like to be talked to."

"Another book fair nut, Lo Ban. Don't worry. What books did he move?"

Lo Ban showed me a Kircher *Mundus Subterraneous* that Armani Suit had moved from one shelf to another. I picked up the volume. "Nothing damaged, Lo Ban," I observed. But over the years, I had learned not to ignore Lo Ban's sixth sense of danger.

Suddenly I noticed it. A faint trace of white powder. Sort of like a light dusting of flour trapped by the nicks and gouges the ages had given to the leather binding. But much more recent.

My own warning light had just come on. Amanda returned with coffee and we all sat down to try to figure out what to do. Fortunately the traffic in the fair was light and nobody came into Lo Ban's booth. "Frankly, Lo Ban," I said, "this doesn't make sense. Somebody is threatening you because you know that somebody wants to take horse into the States. You don't know who, but de Bruin is involved. That old Nazi is well connected. Be careful. And then there's Armani Suit and the books."

"So you believe me about that guy?" Lo Ban sounded relieved. I didn't tell him about the powder on his book.

The fair was really quiet now. A lot of the dealers had abandoned their booths and were off at the bar discussing their day's kill.

I had a clear view of the entry and I saw them come in. Four cops and two dogs. Sniffer dogs. It was one of the few times I was grateful for an empty floor at a book fair.

"Amanda," I said very quietly, "Take this book over to de Hooch's booth and put it under his counter. Be very casual." I gave her the Kircher. Lo Ban had bought it from de Hooch earlier in the fair and it still had de Hooch's inventory and price code in it.

Lo Ban didn't comment, protest, or question. Amanda ambled to de Hooch's unattended booth and left the book, paused to examine a few items as though browsing, and wandered back. A cool operation. Amanda knew her stuff.

In the meantime, I had taken a couple of her cigarettes and spread the tobacco on the carpet in Lo Ban's booth. A few shreds went onto the bookshelves and the filters into the trashcan. For once, I was glad she still smoked. Then we sat and waited. I took down one volume of *The Mustard Seed Garden* and played bookbuyer. I didn't play long.

Cops and dogs headed straight for Lo Ban's booth. A small crowd of dealers followed them, wondering what was the trouble. I thought I saw a flicker of gloat wash across de Hooch's face, but wasn't certain. *No matter,* I thought.

"Please stand outside the booth." The cops were polite. Cops and dogs seemed to know where to go and they went directly to the shelf where the Kircher had been. The dogs, though, had taken a few sniffs of the carpet and hadn't

Under Cover

liked the tobacco. Now they sniffed more of it on the shelf. They lost some of their enthusiasm. "Nothing here!" they signaled to their masters.

Cops and dogs stood in the aisle. The cops seemed puzzled, but ready to leave. I walked up to the cops and became an indignant fair-goer. "I travel four thousand miles to go to this fair and then dogs chase me away from the books." As I berated the cops, I gradually moved closer to de Hooch's booth; the cops and dogs went with me, not realizing they were being led. I leaned against the post by the entrance to de Hooch's booth. I couldn't really get any closer and had to hope that the dogs were good. They were. No tobacco here. Just some good Laos heroin rubbed onto the cover of the Kircher. And they found it.

There was a scuffle. Face purple with rage, de Hooch was shouting and thrashing. He was remarkably strong but they 'cuffed him and took him away. It took a while for the fair to quiet down; nobody quite knew what had happened and we decided that we "didn't know from nuttin." Fortunately, we closed early that night.

Later in the evening, Lo Ban, Amanda and I were having dinner at de Kooning van Siam, our favorite Thai restaurant in Amsterdam. We were in a private room, lavishly appointed and far from the noisy diners in the main restaurant. We knew from experience that we could talk freely in this room.

"It still doesn't make sense." Lo Ban was puzzled. "Why tell me about the drug caper and then set me up?"

Just then, the owner entered. "Will you see this man?" he asked as de Bruin walked in from behind him. In the oblique light, de Bruin suddenly looked his ninety years.

He seemed to have deflated, and his skin hung like last week's birthday balloon.

Lo Ban, Amanda, and I didn't need to even glance at each other. I stood up and pulled out a chair for de Bruin. The owner departed as noiselessly as he had entered and we were left in the presence of one of the last of Europe's unfettered Nazis. I stood behind and a little to the side of de Bruin. Just a precaution.

"It is not necessary. You can sit down, please," said de Bruin to me in a very tired voice. "It is over."

"The whole story, de Bruin." It was Amanda who spoke. So quietly it was barely above the whisper of the ceiling fan, but the authority in her voice would have made MacArthur salute.

"You guys *are* good." De Bruin even smiled. "Yes, very good. That was a beautiful operation today. And I thought your skills were a legend."

"De Bruin, I know you have friends, but if you ever mess with us, you'll really learn about legends." I was getting angry.

"Let me continue," said de Bruin. "They've pulled my protection. For fifty years I give them help and now the bastards stop helping me. Wiesenthal's gotten the OK and he's coming. I'm going to die in jail." The old Nazi cringed. "No!" he slammed down his hand. "I shall not!"

"You framed me." Lo Ban was angry. "Why?"

"De Hooch is running drugs for the CIA. He began in Laos when he worked for Air America. I helped them with my contacts in Jakarta and Indonesia. That bought me protection again. Now, after fifty years they're dumping me. I have nothing more to sell them. And they promised never to dump me. I know about your backgrounds. If they got you for the drugs they would eventually get to de Hooch. That's why I used his book." The old Nazi sighed. "The way you flipped that operation and set him up was amazing. They arrested him. His whole house was full of heroin. They got it all. He's done for. They all are. That'll teach them to dump me."

De Bruin was getting agitated. I had lost my appetite. *"Und ganz am Erde heult jeder Nazi. Raus, Schwanzkopf!"* De Bruin shuddered. Hearing German had struck a chord. He got to his feet and raised his arm in silent salute. Then he was gone.

"It ain't over," said Amanda. We finished our meal in silence.

The next day was the final day of the Amsterdam Book Fair. Lo Ban got there early to tidy up his booth. de Hooch's booth already had been removed. There wasn't even a scar. The edentulous place in the line of booths had been closed by adroit readjustment of the adjoining booths. I noted that old Ignacio Sanscouvert had enlarged his display of plates and leaves from the many books he had broken over the years.

The floor was buzzing with stories and rumors about de Hooch. Most of the dealers seemed more interested in gossip than in trade. I didn't say much. I was worried about the Nazis. I was also worried about the CIA. And I had an uncomfortable suspicion that there was going to be more trouble.

I was right.

They found de Bruin in the Prinsen Gracht, the canal that runs just in front of Anne Frank's house. His body had gotten snagged on some old bicycles rotting in the canal and they fished him out. He was face down and there were no marks on him.

"Wiesenthal got cheated." said Lo Ban when he heard of the old Nazi's death.

We were all glad when the fair closed and we could leave. The wonderful old city of Amsterdam had taken on an unpleasantness that seemed to invade our very beings. We packed quickly.

Just before Lo Ban left Amsterdam he learned that the cops had found over 100 kilos of heroin in de Hooch's house. This was worrisome. If de Hooch really had been Air America, as the old Nazi claimed, then the drugs were CIA drugs and they were going to be upset at losing them.

We all tried to forget, or at least suppress, the events of our Amsterdam trip. Lo Ban and Amanda, after getting back to America, went to Colorado for some spring skiing. I spent a week in Vermont feverishly getting out a catalogue. I wanted to get it out early so that I still had time for a quick trip to Vienna before the New York Book Fair in late April. All that mayhem in Amsterdam was unsettling and I needed to do some serious bookselling to clear my head.

The catalogue was at the printer's when I got the fax from Lo Ban. De Hooch had been found hanged in his jail cell. It was an outside job. "Let's send a wreath," suggested Lo Ban, but I vetoed that idea.

"Let's keep a low profile." That was my suggestion. I'd done some checking on my own and some of my old flying buddies had indeed confirmed the Nazi's story. The late de Hooch had been Air America. And that meant the CIA was somewhere near. And probably pissed at having lost their drugs.

I worked hard the next few weeks and even got some housecleaning done. A large accumulation of defective or otherwise unsalable maps were packed off to the London auction houses. Much repaired, heavily bleached, and then recolored with a garish palette, these maps would do well at the sales. This is where novices buy their maps and they think that everything sold there is a bargain.

My catalogue came out and did well. Over half the items sold within the first week.

"This is going to be a good spring," I thought to myself as I took some of my foreign orders to the little post office in Norwich, Vermont.

The postal clerk was new and I did not recognize her. She dealt with my packages with assurance and it was clear that she was used to foreign addresses. Never before had this little post office had a clerk completely unknown to me. The town was too small for that to happen, but I didn't think much of it. I paid with some large notes and put the change back into my wallet as I left the building. Between two of the twenties she gave me as change was a business card. It was from the de Kooning van Siam restaurant in Amsterdam. I was puzzled, especially when I noted the Chinese characters on the back. Roughly translated they said "Be careful."

Pale Horse

An honourable murderer, if you will;
For naught did I hate, but all in honour.
— *Othello* act 5, sc.2. (Shakespeare)

In the midst of all the activity resulting from my new catalogue, I got a telephone call from someone named Reiner Lügner, who identified himself as a collector of old prints and maps of Spain. Did I have any? I didn't know Reiner but I did know maps of Spain. And I had some in stock. Some great ones, in fact. Reiner was calling from Boston and wanted to drive up the next day. I gave him directions. There was nothing unusual about this; the trip from Boston is a simple, quick, drive. My office is a bit over two hours from downtown Boston and many collectors make the drive to see me.

I, like most dealers, can usually tell a lot about new customers within minutes of meeting them. Their income level, education, and level of sophistication. With Reiner I could do very little. He was a generic individual. Anonymous German accent, with perhaps a bit of Viennese intonation. He deftly turned away my polite, friendly questions about what he was doing visiting Boston; about his collection; about other dealers with whom he did business. Most collectors are willing to provide this

71

information in a friendly non-confrontational way. It establishes their *bona fides* and says to the new dealer, "I'm all right, Jack." Moreover, if they've done business with other serious dealers it establishes their credit.

The only thing I could tell for certain about Reiner was that he didn't know much about maps. He selected, despite my well-meaning advice, two hideous specimens. These heavily restored, unimportant maps were going to be consigned to the London auctions. I occasionally find myself saddled with some really bad maps — they come creeping in on bulk deals — that I don't dare even show to bad private clients. The London auction houses are happy to get them: they can sell them readily to collectors, frantically bidding against each other. Or at least bidding against Sir Chandelier. Firm in their knowledge that auction houses have the answer to a teenage prayer, such collectors form the backbone of the auction house's middle range clients. Disdaining the chance to buy a map for $500 in a dealer's showroom, they froth at the mouth for a chance to buy the same thing for a thousand at an auction!

The two Spain maps were in this category. They were typical of the heavily restored and remade maps sold on the continent. "Continentalized" is how we refer to them in the trade. And Reiner bought them. For cash. I felt badly, for to sell this quality to a private client can only mean disaster in the long run. But he wouldn't listen. In the meantime, he was clearly interviewing me. Casually dropped questions, casual long pregnant pauses that I was supposed to fill in. And fill in I did. Once I figured out what he was doing, I filled him in with all sorts of subtle misinformation. Just an old habit of mine.

After Reiner left I made a quick trip into Hanover to pick up a map list I had had printed at the Kwikie Kopie Shoppie. Counter service was slow and I waited, looking idly out the window. Then I saw them. At the pay telephone. Reiner Lügner was talking and next to him, waiting patiently, was a shorter person. Armani Suit himself. I had last seen Armani Suit in Amsterdam, when Lo Ban and I suspected him of planting the heroin in Lo Ban's booth.

I forgot about my list of maps and the slow counter service. This was far more interesting. I went out to the bank of pay phones.

"Tag, Reiner! Was machen Sie hier?" I greeted him warmly. "You should have asked me — you could have used my office phone." Reiner was clearly uncomfortable. I introduced myself to Armani Suit but he just mumbled back at me. I didn't get his name. "And by the way, Reiner, I forgot to tell you in the office. I have a wonderful copy of the Schedel woodblock *Todentanz*. I must demonstrate (I used the term "demonstrate" instead of "show" deliberately) it to you some day." I smiled broadly at him and at his discomfort. Armani Suit had walked away, not wanting to get into a conversation with me. Reiner mumbled something about his rental car and excused himself. He unconsciously did a little heel-click. I pretended not to notice.

My map list was ready and this time I didn't have to wait in line at the Kwikie Kopie Shoppie to pick it up. I hurried back with it to my office across the Connecticut River to finish the rest of the mailing.

73

The telephone was ringing as I entered the office. It was, luckily, Lo Ban, telephoning from Colorado.

"Manasek, watch out. They're after us." Someone had skied past Lo Ban on the slopes and shot at him. The bullet missed and Lo Ban took control. "They'll find the shooter in a month or so," said Lo Ban, "when the edelweiss blooms. I got into his room and found out who he is, or claims to be. A neoNazi thug. Or was." Lo Ban had not gone soft, nor had he lost his touch. It must have surprised the Nazi enormously when he realized just how much he had underestimated Lo Ban. His final surprise.

Amanda Chin went to Hong Kong after the ski trail assassination attempt. "She always goes there to recover," said Lo Ban. "I don't know where she'll go once it goes communist."

I invited Lo Ban to Vermont so we could figure this thing out. "This is amazing stuff, Lo Ban," I said as we were sipping drinks in the bar at the Norwich Inn in Vermont. The Inn would be perfect if only they got proper martini glasses. Sally Johnson, the proprietress, came over to the bar to say "hello" and we had a pleasant chat. Lo Ban had not been here for a few years and he enjoyed seeing Sally again. We were looking over the folder of papers he had removed from the assassin's room. Sally looked down at them and discreetly excused herself.

"These guys are running a drug ring. It looks like de Bruin found out and knew too much." Lo Ban was pensive. "I wish he hadn't gotten us involved," I said. "This still makes no sense. If de Hooch was Air America, then he's CIA. CIA and Nazis make sense. But why get the Nazis involved in drug-running? Lo Ban, it looks like we're out of retirement!"

"No, old friend. This is too big. We don't have the right connections any more, we have no back up." Lo Ban was right. We should leave it alone.

But it wouldn't leave *us* alone.

Lo Ban and I agreed that we wouldn't pursue Reiner or Armani Suit. Finding them would be too difficult and there didn't seem to be anything in it for us. It didn't make sense that they had come here to see me. We could not understand why they had wanted to case my office. Anyone who knew me knew that this was a legitimate antiquary's office; it was not an operations base. Nor had it ever been one. It was common knowledge throughout the world that I was out of operations. At least officially. Hopefully these palookas would realize that we didn't want to mess with them and they would leave us alone. Hopefully.

With both de Hooch and de Bruin dead, the connection between books and heroin seemed, to us, to be over. But then, I got a package in the mail. Shipped from Frankfurt, with the return address of a notable dealer, the packet arrived in the regular mail, uninsured and uncertified. I was surprised because I hadn't ordered anything from this dealer, nor did it have his usual printed shipping label. Even so, I did not suspect anything. The wrapping looked right and the book was wrapped in a plastic bag. But something had leaked out of the book and was clinging to the inside of the plastic bag. A white powder.

I didn't open the bag nor disturb the packing any more than I had already. "Cover yourself, Manasek," I thought. And I did. In the most open and direct way I could think of. I called the local police department. Sleepy little Norwich, Vermont would have to get involved. And my ass would be covered.

75

Chief Koslewski sat down in my office. "Never been here before." He looked about, clearly curious about his surroundings. "How old are these?" He pointed to a pile of maps overflowing a corner of a desk. "About 1600 or so," I answered. He whistled.

"I get around a lot, chief." I began to explain my call to him. "And I know, from some friends, that there have been attempts to smuggle heroin into this country in old books. Particularly through Amsterdam. I was in Amsterdam a while ago when something like that happened, but I don't know much more than that."

The chief was dubious. "I know about drugs in old books. But I'm not sure why it should involve you." Chief Dubious became Chief Suspicious. "What else do you know about it? Why do you suspect this book has heroin in it?" He pointed to the little volume wrapped in plastic.

"I don't know that it does, but if it does, I don't want to be suspected of drug-running. Or anything else. I did not order this book and I doubt that it's from the dealer whose name appears on the label. You take it and do with it what you want. I just want it out of here. If it's heroin you deal with it, if not then it doesn't matter."

Just then the telephone rang. "Hello, Frank, this is Les."

It was indeed Les, my flying buddy from the Old Days. Les told me he was in the area and that he wanted us to get together for a drink. "Sounds good," I said, just a bit concerned that yet another coincidence was happening. Les was staying at the Hanover Inn and he gave me his room number. "Stop by the room first, then we'll go have a drink."

"Be over in an hour, Les. Sounds good."

76

"Great. See you then. Over and out."

My neck hair stood up and that old feeling came over me. It was a setup. An old pilot like Les would never say "over and out." That's the stuff of B movies and it's what amateurs *think* pilots say. But we don't. And Les was letting me know something was up at his end. And it wasn't bottoms.

I spent the next twenty minutes filling in chief Koslewski and hoping that he'd buy the story. We had to act fast. I was certain that Les was in trouble and that I couldn't handle it myself. Koslewski bought the story. I think he wasn't sure that it was worth pursuing, but I am also sure that he was bored with being chief in Norwich, where stray dogs are the worst offenders and where real crime hadn't yet been invented.

There wasn't time to get the Hanover police involved. They were a much larger department and it would take forever to convince anyone that this wasn't just a Dartmouth student prank. Koslewski and I decided to do this as a private job. If it turned out to be big stuff it wouldn't matter and if it was a prank it wouldn't matter either. Deep down inside, I think that Koslewski really suspected that this was just a big lark, but that somehow I might be involved in something bigger and he would get to make a big bust. Biggest in Norwich's history.

But Koslewski chickened out when we got to the Hanover Inn.

"Really got to get the locals involved." He was concerned that he was treading on thin legal ice. "I really shouldn't be here."

"So much for you," I thought. I picked up the lobby telephone and dialed Les' room. He answered in a slightly quavering voice.

"I'm sorry to disturb you, sir," I pretended to be the manager. "We have a leak in the bathroom in the room above yours and we can't find the shut-off valve for that room. We have to get into yours to get at the master valve in the closet wall. I'm terribly sorry, but a plumber will be there in a few minutes. Again, my apologies and we will have you as our dinner guest tonight."

I sprinted up the stairs before Les and his captors could digest that call and make a plan. A wad of wet tissue stuck to the door peephole and prevented them from looking out at me as I knocked on the door. "Plumber! Emergency call!"

"You can't come in!" A strange voice answered. I heard a window open and I knocked again. A bit more forcefully. The door opened and a head was thrust out. It was Reiner. I grabbed him quickly and he didn't even utter a final sound. Except perhaps for a low gurgle as I pushed him backwards into the room. The window was open and I saw Armani Suit go down the fire escape. Les was tied to a chair but seemed to be otherwise all right. Reiner wasn't and he didn't move. A trickle of blood oozed from his ear.

"You don't know from nothing, Les. Just stay tied up — don't get loose!" I disappeared down the hall and down the stairs into the lobby. Koslewski was still on the phone, finishing his call to the Hanover police. "They're on the way," he said as he hung up.

"Good," I replied. "I think we may need backup on this one. I don't want to mess with those guys alone."

Twenty minutes later a bored young lad in a policeman's suit showed up. "Where's the trouble?"

Koslewski had a lot of explaining to do when the detectives were through with the room where they found Les tied to a chair, an open window and Reiner dead on the floor with a broken neck. Koslewski was certain I had been with him all evening and Les was an experienced hand at all this. Nobody learned nuttin'. Les convinced the police he was a victim of a burglary attempt that had gone bad when he surprised the burglars in his room.

"Armani Suit is dead," said Lo Ban, when he telephoned me a day later. Lo Ban had called earlier to congratulate me on the caper. "He was found in a fleabag residence hotel in Chicago's Hyde Park district. OD'd on heroin."

"Someone got him, Lo Ban," I said, more than somewhat worried. "He was a trafficker, not a user. De Hooch's old ring is still in operation. I think they sent me that book to try to frame me. They'll try again."

"Maybe not, old friend. They're dropping like flies. We might not be worth it."

I certainly hoped so, as I packed my bag. I still had time for a quick trip to Vienna before the New York fair. I looked forward to letting the Bristol Hotel take care of my needs while the Norwich rumor mill churned its way through yet another Vermont mud season.

Back Seat Blues

Il n'y a guère d'homme assez habile pour connaître tout le mal qu'il
fait.
— *Maximes* 269. Duc de la Rochefoucauld (1678)

Adrian was big. Bloated, offensive, and arrogant. Always
pushing people around. He liked nothing better than to
humiliate someone vulnerable. Ranting at his staff, making
his driver wait in the rain, and doing his best to make people
feel inferior and ill at ease. Physically he was a sort of Nero
Wolfe character; indeed he even grew orchids. He liked to
lounge around his house in silk pyjamas and dressing gown,
their colors making his doughy face even more pallid. An
aging queen, decaying with thermodynamic certainty and
irreversibility; increasing in impotent rage in a house filled
with splendid things that, unlike he, increased their
splendor with their age. A veritable cabinet, the house was
stuffed with treasures ranging from classical antiquity to
great artifacts from the early years of our country to old
master paintings to rare natural history specimens. And all
collected by being overbearing, by bullying dealers,
cheating them, and threatening them. Dealers always tried
to gain his favor; they knew he could afford to buy
expensive items and their hopes sprang eternal. As did the
inevitable disappointment when they tried either to get

81

paid or get their goods back. This New England Goebbels defiled the very beauty of his possessions by possessing them. And I was on my way to see him.

Although he didn't know it and I never told him, he and I had the same Alma Mater. Adrian had hinted he might give some maps to our Library (although nobody really believed it) and I was asked to do the appraisal. Just in case. I suspect I was the only person who would take on that unpleasant job. I had never tried to disguise my contempt for him and never tried to sell him anything. I didn't need his business and didn't want it. He knew it and hated me for it. I was probably the only dealer around who wouldn't kowtow and he couldn't stand it. I had him on a cash-only leash and enforced it.

I had last seen him a few years ago when he came into my Hanover office and decided he wanted an Ortelius world map. "Cash?" He feigned disbelief. "Look, Mr. Dealer, I'm going to take this map and you're going to send me an invoice. That's what you're going to do!" He glared and bellowed and pressured.

"Adrian, take that map out the door without paying first and it's grand larceny." He knew I meant it.

This is the kind of guy with whom I was now going to have to spend a few hours. But I owed the library a favor. A big one. Now, they're gonna owe me one. A big one.

Adrian lived in northeastern New Hampshire and I had to cross the White Mountains to get there. It was still early in the day and I had allowed a lot of extra time for the trip. The route over the White Mountains was a two-lane highway that was often fog-shrouded in the autumn mornings, when wisps of vapor connected the tall pines with the macadam roadway. More dangerous were the dense, dank layers of fog that filled the little dips and depressions as the road wandered between the hills. Sometimes complete whiteouts lurked unexpectedly just around the bend. I had anticipated all this and allowed a lot of extra time.

Part-way there, I stopped for coffee at a small-town diner. The coffee was terrible. I finished one cup but didn't bother with a second cup. The doughnut was worse. I finished one bite but didn't bother with a second. The waitress was slow and I now waited at the cash register to pay the bill. As I stood there looking and waiting I suddenly noticed the map hanging on the wall behind the register. It was a roller map, one of those backed with linen and used in schools or public buildings. I peered over the register and squinted at the map. It looked familiar and it was. It was an Osgood Carleton map of Massachusetts. And hanging on the wall behind the register of a shabby diner!

"Everything OK?" She took my check and my ten-dollar bill.

"Oh, sure." I wasn't about to argue with her when there was a Carleton map on the wall! "What's with the map on the wall?"

"Husband's." She hardly answered.

"Is he around?"

"Seth!" Great loud voice. Seth came shuffling in.

"I like that map. It looks very nice. Is it for sale?"

"I just bought it from the antique shop down the road. Guy's got a couple more. Sure. I'll sell it. I like it, but it's gonna get greasy hanging here. I put a lot of stuff back here on the wall and you'd be surprised at how much I sell!"

"How much?"

"I paid a hundred. How about a buck-and-a-half?"

"Done!" I took a hundred fifty out of my wallet and handed it to him. He rolled up the map and handed it over the counter to me. "Where's this shop that has more maps?"

"Just down the road about a mile and a half. It's on the right. Sign says 'Rare Books and Magazines' He's got a lot of big old maps."

"Thanks." I walked out with my map under my arm. It was in nice condition, even the rollers were good, with original finials and clean, black paint. Had he asked me for an offer I would have said three grand.

A mile and a half down the road I saw the sign and stopped. The shop was in a small garage; wood-grain vinyl siding sagging, light on and door ajar.

"Hello!" I called and walked in. "Hello!"

No answer. I looked around but still saw no one. It was cold and damp; the door had evidently been open a while and the fog had rolled in and out, leaving its cold, clammy calling card. Nobody was here. Untended shops such as this are not uncommon in rural New England and I wandered about, trying to find the maps. Roller maps, as these, are usually stuck in boxes or left leaning in corners. They are big and should be obvious. Hopefully by the time I found them, the owner would be back.

But I had no luck. No maps and no owner. I thought I'd leave him a note and stop in on my way home.

There was a small desk in the corner, a notepad and pencil on top of a pile of bills and old book catalogues. The notepad had a list of maps. Yesterday's date was on the top and the last entry was not finished, as though the writer was interrupted at his task. I looked at the list more carefully. He had quite some maps, this out-of-the-way dealer!

Three Osgood Carleton maps were listed; Maine, Massachusetts, United States. He had a John Mitchell *America* and an Aaron Arrowsmith *North America* as well as the Arrowsmith *Africa*. These were noted as having full hand color! All noted as being in fine condition. Then there was a 1733 Popple map. He had just begun writing down a Blaeu world roller map when the entry stopped.

Next to the pad was a newly opened box of business cards. I snooped some more and saw that they had just been delivered - the date on the invoice was yesterday's. I helped myself to one of the cards. This was someone I would have to telephone as soon as I was done with the appraisal.

I was about to leave when I noticed the blood. It was on the concrete floor and seemed to be coming from under a pile of old *National Geographic* magazines. The *Geographics* were just dumped against the wall; not stacked, but thrown down in no order. And blood was coming from under them. I kicked a few aside and saw the body.

The town constable was there within a few minutes; state police a little later. The owner was indeed under the pile of *Geographics*, his head still had the hatchet stuck in it. No struggle; the cops didn't think it was robbery. He had about fifty bucks in the till.

"Find those maps." I had finished with my statement and now was pointing to the penciled list on the desk. "They're not here now and they were yesterday."

"Nobody would kill him for a few old maps," laughed the Trooper. "This wasn't robbery. This guy sells five-dollar books!"

"Yep, and fifty thousand-dollar maps."

I was an hour late for my meeting with Adrian. He was furious. "You piece of shit," he bellowed as his dressing gown flapped open. "I told you to be here at one. Who do you think you are? When I say one I mean one!" I stood there and let him rant. This metamorphosed toad belly was quivering and squinting, as though unused to the daylight. "Get the hell out of here. Don't come back." He was so angry that some color had actually returned to his face. The thin skin had lost its groin-like appearance and become ruddy, tiny blood vessels showing through.

"Well, that's that," I thought profoundly, as I backed out. No point in trying to explain.

"And get your goddamn car out of the driveway!"

As I walked down the driveway to get into my car, I passed his. His big Lincoln, a behemoth from an earlier day, was as bloated as its owner. I glanced inside, fleetingly, as I walked by. The back seat had several roller maps on it and there were more on the floor. I saw the title on a partially unrolled one. Next to it was one of the newly printed business cards from the murdered dealer.

I hurried to my car, drove out as fast as possible and, once on the highway, picked up the telephone off the cradle. It was still hard to get the cops interested in a bunch of old maps, but they finally understood.

The library was going to have to do without a few more maps. But I could work the story for a martini or two at the club.

Curiosity pulled me back to the Rare Book and Magazine shop on my way home. The police were long gone; a few women, evidently neighbors, were standing about, talking and laughing. I pulled into the driveway and introduced myself.

"I'm the wife," said one of the women. She didn't look overly concerned. Standing there, her ample arms folded defiantly, her faded print dress sagging slightly to one side, she did not appear to be in mourning.

In the background I could make out "domestic abuse," "wife beater," and sundry other comments. The neighborhood women evidently were there to support "the wife."

"Listen," "the wife" said earnestly to me. "You know this Adrian guy. Cops said so." She made an obscene gesture. "The bastid would always cheat my husband. Not pay him. Threaten him. Make his goddamn life miserable. Then my old man would take it out on me. I hate both them bastids."

"But you gave Adrian a present yesterday, Maggie!" One of the women said this and everyone, including Maggie, laughed. Hardly a mourners' circle.

Maggie winked a sly eye at me. "His goddamn car window was open."

Fragmented Nobles

All are but parts of one stupendous whole,
Whose body, Nature is, and God the soul.
— *An Essay on Man*, Epistle 1 (Alexander Pope, 1733)

In addition to maps and atlases, I deal with loose, individual leaves from old books and manuscripts. There are still a lot of fragments of important early printing around, partial or defective volumes, and one can salvage bits and pieces from them and turn a profit.

Books printed before 1500 are known as *incunables*, a word referring to the cradle, or infancy of printing. These books have a very special mystique about them and there is a curious practice of collecting individual leaves from them. Indeed, there are books that consist of collections of individual leaves from incunabula. There are also books written about old books, particularly incunabula, that contain, as part of the charm of the new work, a separate leaf from the incunable.

Some dealers, such as the notorious Ignacio Sanscouvert, are quite robust dismemberers and always have a large stock of individual pages. Others, myself included, do not have razors quite as promiscuous and don't practice *codex interruptus* with quite the same vigor. Nonetheless, when the opportunity arises, we will buy and sell individual leaves.

Perhaps the most treasured of all such leaves are those from the Gutenberg Bible, the first Western printed book.

Some decades ago, the well-known New York dealer, Gabriel Wells, took apart a fragment of a Gutenberg Bible and sold the leaves individually. Some of them were nicely bound with an essay by A. Edward Newton entitled *A Noble Fragment*. I don't remember how many leaves were marketed, but for many years they were selling at around $3000. Each. Recently the price has jumped and they seem to have found a new plateau at around fifteen to twenty thousand. Each. Clearly, Gutenberg Bible leaves had become valuable as well as significant items. I was always intrigued by these leaves, but I never owned any. Over the years, I saw several sold at New York's Swann Galleries and, more recently, at Christie's, but I was never impressed with them and didn't want to fight it out on the auction floor with some rabid collector, or the ubiquitous Herr Mauer, or Sir Chandelier, one of whom is present at most sales. Nonetheless, like most dealers, I had noted the leaves' existence and would be more than willing to add them to my inventory if I could get them at the right price.

That opportunity presented itself.

I was wiling away some time wandering around the Ephemera Fair near Hartford Connecticut. I used to find good things at these fairs, but they had, in recent years, yielded precious little for my inventory. This was a particularly dry one and I was resigned to finding nothing. One dealer had a few old vellum antiphonal leaves in dreadful condition and priced very high. I was flipping through them when I saw two framed leaves. Printed leaves. Just stuck behind glass, they were not matted, so I could see their margins and edges. They looked like Gutenbergs to me and a quickly sneaked look through a magnifying glass convinced me they were not from the reprint facsimile edition. At sixty bucks for the pair, the downside risk was about right.

The two leaves were indeed Gutenbergs and I had no trouble selling them quickly. About a month later, at the Washington, D.C. book fair, I told the story to a group of dealers who were sitting around waiting for the end of a long, boring day. We speculated on the origin of these rogue leaves, since close examination showed they were not from the Gabriel Wells fragment.

Just before the fair closed for the day, the long sepulchral aisles devoid of customers, yielded one live body. It was Lo Ban, my old friend and colleague, who came to my booth and tossed a page on my counter.

"Is this one, also?" he asked.

"Yes, it is." This one wasn't behind glass and I could tell immediately.

Lo Ban quickly returned with two more. "Two hundred bucks a pop," he said, smiling broadly.

"Something's wrong, Lo Ban," I said. "There can't be this many *Noble Fragment* leaves that suddenly lost their provenance. All of a sudden it seems that nobody knows what these things are and they turn up in weird places. What are the odds of finding five Gutenberg leaves with dealers who don't know them from a hole in the ground? I think they have to be new to the market and somebody's selling them who doesn't know what they are."

"You mean somebody's breaking a Gutenberg bible? You're nuts," Lo Ban snorted.

Meanwhile, I looked at Lo Ban's purchases closely. There were traces of pencil marks in the lower corners of both. "Let me take these back to Vermont with me. I want to look at this more closely in my lab." Lo Ban agreed.

Whoever had erased the pencil had done a good job. My regular lights, magnifiers, and filters didn't help. Dark field illumination, which often shows broken fibers, such as those caused by erasures, didn't help. Finally when I used coherent light, I could make out part of the markings. I could see the number 600 and either "pts" or "pta."

"They're Spanish, Lo Ban," I said into the telephone. "If I'm right, they cost 600 pesetas. About five bucks. Somebody in Spain is breaking a Gutenberg and he doesn't know what he's got!"

"But we do and we're going to find it, right?" I heard a faint click on the line. "It's OK, Manasek, just Amanda. She's already packing."

Two days later, our old friend and companion, Maria de Cordova, met us at the airport in Madrid and drove us to Toledo where she currently lived. I stayed with Maria in Toledo. We had a lot of catching up to do. Lo Ban and Amanda stayed in the Hotel Cardenal, that wondrous paean to his mistress that the old cardinal had built into the city wall by the Hapsburg Gate.

It was good to be back again in Spain. The four of us celebrated our reunion with a wonderful meal served in the courtyard of the Cardenal. The warm Spanish night, filled with swallows, descended upon us as we allowed ourselves the luxury of reminiscing. "The habit of old people," Lo Ban once remarked.

We brought up the subject of the Gutenberg leaves. "Sooner or later stuff like this winds up in the Rastro." Maria was right. A good place to start our search would be in the Rastro, Madrid's giant flea market.

The evening had grown chilly when we called it a night. Amanda and Lo Ban walked up the steps to the hotel entrance and Maria and I walked out the darkened gate. "It's been a long time, Paco. Glad you're here." She squeezed my hand.

The next morning, the four of us took the train back to Madrid. We didn't talk much. In many ways it was a poignant trip; many such trips had preceded this one, each taking us into a new adventure. This one wasn't dangerous; earlier ones had been, and some of our companions of those earlier rides were no longer here. I suspect we each thought of them on this train ride, but we didn't discuss it. Not overtly. We had done enough together not to need speech to share such thoughts.

The four of us split up and worked the Rastro separately. The crowds got thicker as the hour advanced, and by late morning it was barely possible to move. A local pickpocket tried to get his hand into my jacket pocket. I let him. When it was in, I pulled the jacket tight. He couldn't get his hand out fast enough and my 200 plus pounds came down firmly on the top of his foot. I felt it break under my heel. The pickpocket let out a shrill scream and fled limping into the crowd. "You'll remember that one," I thought.

The crowds remained thick and the search unpleasant, but we kept at it until two o'clock when we met, as agreed, at the little restaurant we used to frequent years ago.

Amanda looked tired. Lo Ban was angry. Someone had picked his jacket pocket and taken his notebook. I told Lo Ban about my pickpocket. I couldn't help smirking just a bit. It didn't improve his mood. Then Maria showed up.

"Tra-la!" she sang out. She put a bunch of stuff down on the table. "Had to buy some of this," she said, pointing to some overpriced derelict vellum antiphonal music sheets, "to get this!" Triumphantly she plunked down four Gutenberg leaves. Each marked, in pencil, 600 pts.

Amanda brightened immeasurably. Lo Ban stopped sulking. "Is this the mother lode?" he asked.

"No." Maria was pretty certain. "This guy just had a few leaves. Mostly he had junk. A whole box of it. The junk and the garbage vellum was priced pretty high. He thought the Gutenberg leaves were a rip-off. I didn't have the heart to dicker with him. He felt sorry for me and gave me a hundred pesetas off each. But he didn't know where the stuff came from. Probably from someone else in the Rastro in a trade. I don't think we'll ever find out."

I studied the junk antiphonal leaves. They were priced in the same handwriting as the Gutenberg leaves. Things began to make sense. "If we assume that the prices penciled on the trashy vellum were put there by the original dealer who sold them, then its got to be Trallejo," I said. "In Barcelona. They're the only people who price vellum this high. Especially this garbage. And that'll be where the Gutenbergs are coming from. It's worth a try."

Fragmented Nobles

We took the night train to Barcelona. The Hotel Colón had rooms; we checked in and still had time to kill. We wandered about the old Barrio waiting for the Trallejo shop to open. Barcelona is a great city; a city with long ties to the New World. A few years earlier I had visited the replica Columbus ships moored in the harbor. Ten minutes on board one of them gave me entirely new respect for the bravery of Columbus and his crew.

By ten, when the Trallejo shop opened, we had our plan ready. Lo Ban, who wasn't known here, would case the place and see if there were any more leaves. He wouldn't buy any if there were. Rather, he would show no interest in them but feign interest only in tourist-trap vellum antiphonal leaves. The Trallejo shop was filled with those. Mostly from the 1600s and early 1700s and labeled with totally spurious dates. They might write "1470" on the bottom of one leaf. Another from the same antiphonal might be labeled "1550." And they sold like hotcakes to the tourists.

We sat in the warm early morning sunshine of the quiet square, looking at the anti-American Basque posters pasted to the walls, waiting for Lo Ban to reappear.

"Bingo!" Lo Ban was deadpan but his voice gave away his enthusiasm. "This is the mother lode. They've got a stack of them. Trallejo hasn't got any idea what this stuff is. The guy has a fucking Gutenberg Bible that he's chopping up and selling for five bucks a page!"

"Lo Ban, please," said Maria sternly, "You're talking about a Bible."

Lo Ban could not read Maria. For all the times we had all worked together, in all the years the two had known

95

each other, Lo Ban could not tell when Maria was serious about things like this. And she loved it. Lo Ban did not answer her. Maria pressed her knee against mine.

"My turn." I got up and went down the street leading to Trallejo's shop. He was glad to see me. "Hola, amigo!" A warm welcome, some strong coffee and the eternal hope that he would sell me a ton of his overpriced stuff. "I need inventory, Juan. I've had a good year and need some vellum music leaves. That's why I came to see you."

I looked around and began making a pile of odd vellum leaves that I would buy. Coming to the pile of Gutenberg leaves, I picked one up. "Nice. What are they?"

"It's from a Spanish Missal. Printed in 1578 in Valencia. Very rare." He lied. "You should buy some."

"Too pricey." I put the leaf down, noting its price of 600 pesetas. Just then Amanda and Maria walked in.

Maria spoke English, in an affected, heavy Spanish accent, to Amanda. "Is this what you were looking for? These ancient music sheets on parchment?"

Amanda, feigning the quintessential tourist, grinned. "Wow! They're great!"

Maria turned to Trallejo and spoke in rapid Spanish. "My friend is American. She looks Chinese but she's American. You know how they are." She bonded with Trallejo. Together, Maria and Amanda looked through the leaves. I continued my search, gradually adding to my pile. Trallejo saw I was buying seriously.

Amanda had picked out a very large vellum sheet. My guess was that it was mid-1700s. Someone had painted garish decorations all along the margins in an unskilled, recent hand. "Wow," gushed Amanda, "I like this! Is it old?"

"About 1500," smiled Trallejo. "Beautiful decoration." Maria translated.

Maria picked up a Gutenberg leaf. "Look at this, Amanda."

"Ugh. That's ugly." Amanda wrinkled her nose. It was a gesture that always, in the past, drove Lo Ban wild, and Maria and I worked hard not to laugh.

I picked up a Gutenberg leaf and turned to Maria. "Le gusta?"

"Sí, but not my American friend. Americans have different tastes."

Trallejo rose to the bait and he was even more determined to sell me the leaves. Amanda interrupted and asked me if I was American.

Trallejo was getting angry. He could smell my sale going bad with all these people butting in. Amanda acted very bored and said she wanted to think about the whole thing and "she would be back." She and Maria left.

"Well, she might be right." I put the leaf back on the counter.

"Americans buy a lot of them," assured Trallejo. "Dealers come and buy them from me and then they sell them for twenty-five dollars each in America." Trallejo lied.

I acted impressed. There were about a dozen on the counter. "How much for all?"

"Five hundred fifty pesetas each."

"If this is all you have, it's not worth my while."

"Wait." Trallejo ran into a back room and emerged with a stack of gatherings. "I have this left. See, I sold a lot!"

I bought all one hundred twenty eight leaves at five hundred forty pesetas each. I also bought the vellum rubbish I had picked out. No reason to get him suspicious. Trallejo wrapped my purchases and I could tell he was very pleased that he had finally unloaded those leaves. We thanked each other formally and I headed out toward the square with the package of Gutenberg leaves and vellum sheets under my arm. Lo Ban, Maria, and Amanda were there. We did not acknowledge each other. I walked by and they kept chatting. Time later for the high-fives; now the utmost caution was in order. Just like the Old Days. We fell into that routine with ease. And it was a good thing we were careful.

Trallejo came running after me. "You forgot your magnifying glass!" He and I chatted a while. My friends wandered off and Trallejo said something not very nice about Amanda and her body. I ignored him.

By the time I got to the Hotel Colón, we were already checked out, bags waiting in the lobby and taxi called. "We're outta here," said Lo Ban. "Night train to Toledo."

We shared guard duty on the ride back to Toledo. One of us was always awake and the package was with us in our compartment. We didn't discuss the leaves or our activities until we got back to Maria's place in Toledo. Then we felt safe enough to open the package.

"One hundred twenty eight leaves." Amanda caressed them.

"Plus the four I got at the Rastro," added Maria. "And at least fifteen grand each."

Lo Ban acted cool. "And the fucking idiot broke a Gutenberg and was selling it for five bucks a pop."

"Please, Lo Ban. Your language. It is a Bible, you know." Maria couldn't resist pulling his chain again and Lo Ban could not tell if she was serious. He tried to look chastised. But only a little bit so he could deny it if needed. Maria pressed her knee against mine.

We divided the pages into four piles and we each selected one pile. We knew each other well enough to know the division was fair.

"I suppose you're leaving soon?" Maria already knew the answer to that one, but didn't press me.

"Will you sell mine for me?" Maria handed me her stack.

Leaving time came all too soon.

Maria and I were finishing our morning coffee when Amanda and Lo Ban arrived. They were off to Hong Kong and I was going to London. We were, once again, about to go our separate ways. However, for a short, final moment we relished the fact some of us had been together again and we wished, silently, that the others could have been here with us. The old group. They were missed. But those of us here were much as we were in the old days, slightly grayer but also wiser and more cunning. And our trust in each other undiminished.

We looked deeply at each other but said nothing — it was as fine a moment as I have ever experienced.

Maria drove us to the airport.

Under Cover

I checked into my flight and Maria walked as far as Passport Control with me. I was carrying our leaves in my attaché case, rolled up. Maria pressed herself to me, kissed me, and gave me a delightful little squeeze.

"When you get to London, say 'hello' to Elizabeth for me, Paco."

The Book of Death

Nati natorum et qui nascentur ab illis.
—Virgil

Xavier Saperstein didn't want to let Lo Ban or me exhibit at the forthcoming International Rare Book Fair. After the killing at last year's fair, Saperstein thought he could finally get rid of us.

"We don't need any of your type here. I don't want any more murders." Saperstein was adamant.

"You want we should rent a suite at the Waldorf, exhibit our Gutenberg leaves, and hold a press conference for why we are there and not here?" Lo Ban had Saperstein cornered. "And we want a double booth right by the door as you come in. On the left."

"I can't do that. Every booth is by impartial honest lottery. You gotta take what you get."

"On the left, Saperstein. I want one on the left side as you come in."

The lighting and location were perfect and as people came into the fair on opening night they turned left and saw our double booth.

The rare book dealers across the aisle from us had a lot of 1950's and 1960's aviation books; next to them were the couple who sold rock'n'roll memorabilia and postcards. The Continental dealers who were next to them vowed never to return again. Saperstein was fielding complaints all night long.

"Nice show, Saperstein! I like the way you manage to mix Little Richard postcards with incunabula. How about a T-shirt booth next year?" Dick Eberhart loved to torment Saperstein. Dick sold medieval manuscripts and this year found himself again at the end of the row next to the men's toilets. He would not be back. Lo Ban jokingly told him that "all it took was a couple of hundred in cash to Saperstein" and a good location was assured. Within an hour the rumor that Saperstein sold booth locations had spread across the floor and Saperstein was pissed.

"Lo Ban, if it was you, I'll kill you."

Lo Ban's face hardened and his eyes became cold and penetrating. "I tell you, not as a threat, but as a statement, never to say that to me again." The low voice sent a shudder through Saperstein. He had heard stories about Lo Ban; vague rumors of his power, of his connections, his wealth and, most of all, his personal cunning. Saperstein said nothing and backed away, bumping into Amanda Chin. He apologized, and as he continued to back away, two centuries fluttered to the floor. Saperstein reflexively bent down to pick them up and the rumor was confirmed.

"I saw those!" cried Dick Eberhart.

Saperstein looked at the two c—notes in his hand and realized what had just happened. He fled in terror.

The opening night was a good one. Lo Ban and I sold fifteen of the Gutenberg leaves. At between fifteen and twenty grand each.

I was going to treat myself to a martini and, before I went to the bar to get it, asked Amanda if she wanted something.

"A gimlet," she answered.

I bought myself the martini and Amanda her gimlet, and then bought a copy of James van Sikle's *Modern Airmanship* at the booth across the aisle. Thirty-five years ago, when I was a young pilot I, read every word in that book. I studied every concept and am still in awe of it as an aviation textbook. I was glad to have a copy again.

Lo Ban was wandering the fair, poking around the various booths looking for oriental books. Each year he found fewer and fewer of them and, although he continued to think of himself as a dealer in Japanese and Chinese books, in reality he sold mostly Western works. Truly great ones, but Western nonetheless. He returned, this time with a small volume, a copy of *Melissa malleficarum* printed in 1511, a little book that had served as a handbook for trying witches and sorcerers. A wonderfully preserved copy in original boards, and Lo Ban had bought it for $3000. He considered it a steal.

"Look at this, Manasek." Lo Ban pointed out one of the back free end pages. "Look at this! A list of names! These are the surnames of known witches and sorcerers and warlocks in Germany in 1500!" I always marveled at Lo Ban's command of languages. Educated in the Far East,

103

Lo Ban spoke at least a dozen languages and, in this case, was able to easily read a manuscript written in Old German. Years ago I tried to compete with his command of languages, but I gave up.

Lo Ban continued. "Look here! A list of prosecutors! Manasek," he continued, "you have no idea how important this list is!"

And, indeed, I didn't. But I would soon find out.

Lo Ban priced the *Melissa* and put it on the shelf next to a work by Luther. It was a fitting juxtaposition; the *Melissa* had a woodblock frontispiece showing demons in hell and the torment they visited upon the souls down there. A deep, dark, foreboding, and glooming frontispiece for a similarly conceived book. I could visualize it on a table in a dark, damp, cold cell, being consulted from time to time by the parties involved. Of course, before I deconstruct too feverishly, we do note that all concerned believed in this stuff and it made perfect sense at the time. The dank culture that gave rise to this must have infected Luther as well. Can anyone document that Martin Luther ever laughed or ever told a joke? I doubt it. At any rate, he was now on the shelf sitting next to the *Melissa*.

A few visitors to the booth looked at the *Melissa*, none seriously.

Until the Germans came. A small group of them entered the booth and looked around. They were talking quietly, in German. About buying some of the Gutenberg leaves. And they were idly browsing the shelves while trying to decide. One of them picked up the *Melissa* and flipped through. He stopped at the manuscript page at the end. It took but a moment for him to become agitated and he called

104

his companions over. They passed the book around, exclaiming.

"Darf ich Ihnen helfen? Möchten Sie was anschauen?" I asked one of them.

He answered in English. "See this page? It lists victims (he pronounced it as "wictims") It lists the families of people these bastards helped destroy. Some of these families had to change their names. Even that didn't work. They were always wictims. We still are. But see here — this last column of names. Those are the names of the prosecutors. Our ancient tormentors."

"We?" But that was three hundred years ago. "Surely it's over."

"Never! We have our own revenge now!."

"Sie sind die ersten 'werewolfen.' Nicht wahr?" Lo Ban had returned and he had listened to the discussion with some interest.

Our visitors blanched. "How do you know this?"

"I didn't know if it was true. I just heard the stories. You are sort of like the avenging angel of death, aren't you?"

The group became sullen. "That is ridiculous." Furtively, they began to drift out of the booth.

"My *Melissa*, please." Lo Ban smiled as he held out his hand to retrieve the book from the last of the Germans to leave the booth. "I am sure you have better lists than these."

"Hitler tried to resurrect the werewolves in the last few days of the Reich." I recalled some dim history. "Didn't he want a band of stealth killers to wage unlimited and eternal warfare on the victors? To come out at night and kill and then hide?"

"Yes," said Lo Ban. "It didn't work. But these guys are different. They've been at it for centuries. Not a one has been caught, yet only a few question their existence. I recognize some of the prosecution names in that book. Those families have lived in terror ever since. Babies butchered, people disappeared, houses burned. Never very much at once, but chronic disaster befell them and never left. Very hard to prove a conspiracy. Or anything, for that matter."

"Take it to court and get laughed at."

"Precisely," said Amanda, returning from a scouting trip around the fair. "But they do exist. There was a double murder in Hong Kong a few years ago that was attributed to the werewolves. A young German student and her traveling companion. We Chinese believed it. Nobody else did at the time."

The thought of the werewolves probably present here, the witch trials, the long smoldering hatred that never died, put a pall over our fair. I had been looking forward to taking some time off after the fair. Perhaps some book buying on the Continent and my usual springtime visit with Veronica in Paris. Indeed, this year Veronica had made it seem very urgent that I get there and I hoped, fervently, that we would not get ourselves involved in any unpleasantness as a result of this ancient feud.

Lo Ban and I discussed the werewolves a bit during the remainder of the fair, but although we tried not to think too much about them, we could not put them out of our minds.

"This is an ancient hatred that has nothing to do any longer with the old trials. It is simply the intolerance of the North Germans that has become a rabid pathology." Lo Ban had come to a decision. His decisions always led to pronouncements. "And they forget their own persecutions. Remember Michael Servetius? Known as Villanova? They burned him because he was Catholic. Years ago, Manasek, before you became involved with our group, I had an experience with some of these people. I didn't know that they were werewolves then, but now I'm certain of it."

When Lo Ban got pensive and reflective like this, I knew better than to interrupt his train of thought. Besides, it was always interesting and provided a very different slant on history. History as viewed by Lo Ban was quite different than history as viewed by, say, me.

"Manasek, fifty or so years ago, my father was traveling in the United States. He was visiting this country to learn about the political and economic system here firsthand. He spent several months in New York and then traveled about the Midwest. Oddly enough he was most interested in the railroad system and methods of food distribution. Eventually he was drawn into Chicago. The stockyards were still operating and he spent a lot of time looking at that operation. He stayed in a hotel in a neighborhood between the yards and the lake, some place called Hyde Park. I've heard it's a festering sewer now. But then it was a modest, but provincial place and he, being Oriental, stuck out like the proverbial sore thumb."

I couldn't resist an interruption. "What did your father do, Lo Ban?" I asked.

"He traveled around, gathering information." Lo Ban answered simply. I didn't ask any more. Clearly Lo Ban was not the first in this line of work.

"At any rate, he tried to keep a low profile and be a good visitor, but it didn't work. There were, at that time, some German families in the neighborhood. They had some connection with a university in the area. This was just after the war and feelings were pretty high. Three little German kids were murdered. These days it wouldn't even be noticed in Hyde Park, but then it was an outrage. I think people thought at first that it was done by Zionists. But my father poked around a bit. It didn't take him long to learn that they were killed by *Germans!* He easily traced a series of similar murders and linked them to a group that had immigrated early in this century. The group was led by an evangelical pastor who was the Ian Paisley of the day. A guy by the name of Schneider. A quick look at newspaper records and a few trips to the library implicated a revenge type of serial killings. Of course, in those days serial killings were not as common as they are now. At any rate, my father thought it was psychopathic and linked it to the group that immigrated with Schneider. The pastor was dead but one of his daughters, Irlinde, was one of the closet fascists during the war. But more important, *she was a werewolf!* My father had discovered a whole list of German kids who were killed in strange ways and he linked them to this group. In those days the world was much smaller and my father's inquiries attracted, unfortunately, a lot of attention.

"The werewolves had a good organization and found out about my father's inquiries. They tried to kill him. Two of them discovered the folly of that, but my father fled the area — this was not his job and not his fight. The Chicago group is, as far as I know, still in existence. I know this because Irlinde Schneider's people got in pretty thick with the CIA and used those contacts to do their own dirty work. I honestly think they are no longer avenging. They probably don't even know the origins of their blood hatred. I think they are pathological killers."

"What a connection, Lo Ban," I struggled with this information. "Does any of this fit in with the Amsterdam gang — the de Bruin crowd?"

"I'm not sure, old friend, and I don't think I want to know." Lo Ban looked pensive. "I want some peace and quiet." Lo Ban was serious. This was not the first time he had said this, and he had backed away from more than one adventure.

"When a group goes rogue and becomes pathologically murderous, they export that murder. It becomes a product, like shoes. I've seen it in the Orient. In the Chicago case, they got tied up with a university in Hyde Park and with the CIA and ultimately they were responsible for the deaths of dozens of Kurdish leaders. That one is a very long story, one that I can't tell you now. But as far as the Amsterdam episodes, I don't know."

When the book fair finally closed Lo Ban and I were able to pack quickly. We had a few Gutenberg leaves left, a few other manuscript leaves, and perhaps another fifty books, all of which fitted nicely into two suitcases. I had, in addition, a small roll of old maps that I tucked under my arm. Lightly loaded, we walked out of the fair. The other dealers, sweating like stevedores, were packing hundreds of used books into old tomato boxes and stacking them skyhigh on dollies, to be pushed down the street to their waiting vans.

We went to Lo Ban's hotel where Amanda was waiting. Lo Ban and I tallied our take and settled up. I left my books and maps with him, picked up my small suitcase that I had stashed in his hotel room, and went outside to get a taxi to the airport.

I was on my way to Paris to meet Veronica. I had just received a postcard from her, a seemingly innocuous card from Rome — a "wishing you were here" type of message. But it was in our old code. She wanted to see me as soon as possible. Something was up.

I no longer get to Paris as often as I used to, so when I do, change is very apparent. It's sort of like filming a city in time-lapse cine and viewing the result — everything happens much faster. One part of this is nice — seeing a city as a living organism that ages, changes, and develops. Another part is sad. I see, with this change in a city I knew, a passage of time, the passage of my life. My old haunts; their change into something else, something that does not any longer include me,; they tell me they have done without me and that they have a less fragile mortality than I.

But the bonds good humans make with each other are not like that. Paris may change, the city may switch flavors, but seeing Veronica was no different than it had ever been. We fell into that comfortable state of being that comes from long acquaintance and long liking of each other. And it was one of my life's great pleasures to sip morning coffee with her, overlooking the mansards of Paris, slick with rain.

It wasn't all beagles and chipmunks, however. Veronica had witnessed a murder in Rome when she was visiting her sister. And the murderer knew who she was. Apparently a small German boy, on holiday with his parents, had been struck on the head with a flowerpot. Veronica was first on the scene and she cradled the dying child in her arms until police arrived. At the police station, where she went to give a statement, Veronica overheard the police speculate about the death. It was the third such child murder the city had seen in the past few months. On her way home, a flowerpot narrowly missed her.

The German connection interested me. We faxed the child's name to Lo Ban to try to match it up with the list of prosecutors in the *Melissa*. "Funny you should do this now," said Lo Ban when he telephoned us. "I checked out the name with the Mormons' genealogy lists and, sure enough, the little kid was a descendant of one of the major prosecutors. Fits in with what we were talking about at the fair, doesn't it?"

I explained to Veronica the story Lo Ban had told me at the book fair. Veronica did not poo-poo the werewolf story as had I. Indeed, she was very concerned about it. Werewolf activity apparently had become too great for some of the victim families in the early part of this century and they fled to the Orient. But they couldn't escape. Most of Veronica's friends in Thailand believed the werewolves existed. Just as Amanda and Lo Ban did. She did not want them after her. "You cannot get away," was her thought.

"Lo Ban and I didn't want to mess with them. His father found out about them and he backed off, too. But now, they're going after one of us. That won't do. Time for us to

111

regroup and remember who we are." I said this very quietly. Veronica pressed my hand.

Another telephone call came from Lo Ban. "Remember that *Melissa*? One of the Germans who looked at it in the New York book fair ordered it. I baited it. Went chumming for werewolves."

"Come clean, Lo Ban. What did you do?"

"I wrote the name of the little kid in Rome on a slip of paper, along with the ancestral name — the surname of the lad's prosecutorial forebear. Then to top it with a cherry I wrote the names "Schneider/Chicago" underneath. I left the slip of paper in the *Melissa* when I sent it to the Germans. That should bring them out."

"I suppose we do the Chicago book fair?" I knew the answer to that one already.

Dead Bookspeak

Those who act in evil are followed by the thought, "I have done wrong," and the memory of the act is stored to work out its inevitable retribution in the following lives. But those who act from good motives are made happy...
— *The Teaching of Buddha*

Chicago is a sports and car town. It is not a book town. It has some hard-core collectors, but only a few and, by and large, they don't buy their books in Chicago. Nonetheless, there is an international book fair in Chicago. It takes more than a bit of hubris to have it here but, invariably, it draws a few dozen of the world's most hopeful dealers.

The fair was no different this year, except that Lo Ban and I were there. We had, a long time ago, sworn never to exhibit at this fair again, but this year didn't count. This time around we had other business to conduct and were confident that our friends, the werewolves who had threatened Veronica, would contact us. With a flowerpot, perhaps.

Lo Ban and I decided to take separate booths. Although it was possible, at these fairs, for two dealers to share a booth, reducing the cost and also making the time pass more quickly, we had decided on individual space. Spread out a bit, we would be less vulnerable. Our booths were on opposite sides of the aisle, locations that cost us an extra five centuries to circumvent the purportedly random lottery used to allocate booth locations at these fairs. This was, after all, Chicago.

Amanda was in Lo Ban's booth. Maria flew in from Madrid and was one of the "sales associates" in my booth. Veronica was located in Jeff Mancevice's booth next to mine. Two of our other friends[1] had been planted in booths near the exits. And we were all armed with .25 automatics. We were all afraid this one was going to be ugly and putting the equalizers in our pockets was reassuring. One way to level a playing field.

Except that we were all a bit older and slower and stiffer, this operation was very like the one we did in Antwerp almost twenty years ago. Then, as now, we had assembled our old group, or what remained of it, and pulled off a "most elegant defensive caper," as one of our Oxford associates remarked over sherry. We were hoping for an encore.

The dread Chicago Book Fair Blahs set in rather early. Opening night drew a smattering of the idle curious and then the aisles became empty. This was both good and bad. We could keep an eye on things more easily, but we were also more vulnerable. Lo Ban in particular was an easier target.

Lo Ban was out getting a sandwich and I was covering his booth. Amanda and I were were sitting and chatting. Amanda was sipping a scotch-on-the-rocks and I was working on what passed for a martini. Suddenly the booth was filled with visitors. The same group that had been to the New York fair and then finally ordered Lo Ban's *Melissa*.

---

1. These individuals are still heavily involved in activities that make it important not to reveal their names.

"Nice to see you again," I smiled, and got up to shake hands all around.

They smiled back and we chatted briefly in German.

"We found a note in the *Melissa* and wanted to ask you about it." They didn't waste any time and any pretense of friendliness was gone. Their smiles were replaced by icy-hard glares. I noticed that they fanned out, forming a military encirclement. I would have been in trouble were I alone. But Amanda had wandered out and Maria had wandered in and now Our Side outflanked Their Side. I don't think they quite yet appreciated the situation.

I picked up the potted plant that Amanda had bought to pretty up the counter. It was in a ceramic pot covered with foil which I peeled back just enough to show the pot. I handed it to the leader. "Fuck with any of us again and you're dead. We know who you are and we will kill you one by one. And after we kill you, I will, personally, kill your families. Thank Irlinde." I spoke very quietly.

The werewolves took a quick look around them and realized they were outflanked. They were military tacticians and could appreciate the fact that we were also. Trapped in a pincers movement, they saw that we had moved in silently and unobtrusively and they knew what this meant.

Lo Ban returned, quite unexpectedly, and he too immediately took in the situation. He stood behind the lead werewolf so that as the killer backed out of the booth he bumped into Lo Ban. Or rather, into the muzzle of his .25 automatic. Lo Ban hissed and the killer paled.

Veronica sidled in from the other direction. She had positioned herself to effectively block their retreat if they tried to flee. The pack of werewolves moved away from Lo Ban and me and edged toward the open aisle, blocked only by Veronica.

Veronica stood in front of them.

"You forgot your flowerpot." The werewolves stopped in their tracks. Veronica let the tip of her .25 show and she silently mouthed a few words. The killers paled. Yet again.

In any decent military exercise one needn't take prisoners or suffer casualties to make a point. If I outflank, outthink, and outmaneuver you, I don't have to kill you to win the engagement. Unless you're stupid. These guys, killer psychopaths that they were, could not be considered stupid.

We won. And they knew it.

We had done more than win this round; we won the battle, if not the war. We had also planted a poison pill in their system, one that would result in terrible disruption to their activities for years to come. By telling them that Irlinde Schneider ratted, we not only guaranteed her destruction by her own comrades, but also the destruction of her influence and that of her closest companions in this game of terror for years to come. Perhaps the "Chicago Chapter" of the werewolves was over.

We sincerely hoped so and hoped, also, that we would not hear from them again. Lo Ban still argued that we should have iced the lot of them but, as Veronica pointed out, that many dead bodies stacked up like cordwood would have raised eyebrows at any book fair. Even in Chicago. Still, the thought was an appealing one, and Maria and I laughed at the thought of the fair organizers explaining away the bodies.

We considered the fair a success, even though we hadn't sold much. No one else had, either. Typical Chicago book fair. Interestingly, the other dealers had noted the activity in our booths and thought we had done a lot of business!

Pack-up was easy and we were out of there less than twenty minutes after the fair closed. Once again we would go our individual ways and spread out over the globe.

Lo Ban and Amanda went to Hong Kong; Maria and Veronica back to the Continent, and I flew to Istanbul and from there took a boat to visit Elizabeth.

Elizabeth was on her Aegean island retreat. This was her hideaway when her world in England got too busy. Which it did all too frequently. Elizabeth had become a painter of some note since our old group disbanded. She and I had developed a very special friendship. Even now, years after her death in a tragic accident, I see her still and her spirit permeates the Aegean. For me, the aeolian winds sing a paean to her forever.

But then, we were so close and alive. Every moment on that island with her was from the gods with whom we shared the place and who looked upon us with kindness. The weekly boat brought us what we needed, including a newspaper. I was then, as now, addicted to the *International Herald Tribune.* Each week the boat brought the previous week's copies of the *IHT.* I would put them in chronological order and read them, one each morning, until the next packet arrived. The world unfolded to us in print, but with a week's delay.

The bits and snippets provided by the *IHT* were enough to give us a flavor of events that surrounded our island, but could not touch us here. There was the familiar stream of catastrophe, overloaded Philippine ferries, Eurocorruption, and American politics. And the weather.

That summer was an uncommonly hot one in the American Midwest. Almost daily, the *IHT* reported of riots and looting in Chicago. The suburbs, newly sprouted on stubbled cornfields, were largely unaffected, but the fetid inner-city areas, such as the notorious Hyde Park district, suffered enormously as howling, raping, mobs smashed their way through the streets, plundering and destroying the storefront churches like synagogues in *Kristallnacht.*

"Glad we're out of there," I said to Elizabeth. She answered with one of her looks that told me very plainly she was still a bit miffed that we had not asked her in on the werewolf caper.

Then, suddenly, another item in the *IHT* caught my attention. In a dismal trailer park in Indiana, not too far from Chicago, a contractor pumping out a septic tank pumped out the remains of a woman tentatively identified as Irlinde Schneider. An abandoned trailer on the site revealed the bodies of three men, as yet unidentified.

"Betcha it's her werewolf buddies. The ones who bought Lo Ban's *Melissa.* They screwed up and paid for it. Saved us the trouble." I tore out the clipping to send to Lo Ban in Hong Kong. Lo Ban, I thought, would enjoy the part about Irlinde in the septic tank. ("Ashes to ashes," is what Lo Ban said, according to Amanda, when he learned the news.)

I had no illusions that this meant the werewolf organizations had been destroyed. They had been around for hundreds of years and survived successfully all earlier attempts to destroy them, and they would almost surely

survive this one. Nonetheless, we had shown our own strength and, hopefully, they would not come after us. I had found my solitude and did not want to lose it. Again.

"Glad you're home, Paco." Elizabeth put her arm around my shoulders. There was goodness and light in the world and I had found it here.

The Mayan Atlas Mystery

Death it can bring,
that kind of mushroom; and, of course,
it's a pretty thing.

— *Issa (1762-1826)*

The PBFA (Provincial Book Fairs Association) is one of the most dynamic book trade groups I know. It was founded by a group of English booksellers who decided that the ABA (Antiquarian Booksellers Association) was not providing the appropriate forum for their business. They felt that the ABA was too upmarket and stuffy in its approach to bookselling. What was needed was frequent and regular book fairs that sold books at all price levels. The Provincial Book Fairs Association is just that — an association whose function is to provide excellent venues for book fairs. For the past decade or so, I have tried to go to as many of the PBFA London fairs as possible. Held in the Russell Hotel, just off Russell Square in Bloomsbury, this fair used to provide my business with a significant percentage of the maps, prints and books that we sold.

121

Several other PBFA fairs were also noteworthy. The Oxford fair was always worth the trip. Not only for the fair itself, but for the wonderful ambiance of, and the memories within, the Old Parsonage Hotel on the Banbury Road. The fair itself was not in the Old Parsonage, it was in the Randolph. But I always stay in the Old Parsonage when I'm in Oxford. And that alone makes the trip worthwhile.

Years ago the London auction houses had frequently provided our firm with choice items. They still do, but only occasionally. The auctions have gone after the retail trade and have captured much of it, bringing with it retail prices. Novices always believe, as an act of faith, that auction prices are, somehow, "wholesale" prices. These are the same folks who also believe the they get the best prices when they sell at auction! That logic has always eluded me, but faith is not logical.

I think it was in 1989. Autumn. I was in London attending the sales when I received a telex from Veronica. She was still in Bangkok but would come to England if I could take some time off from work.

Veronica and I agreed to meet at the Old Parsonage Hotel in Oxford, after I was finished with the round of London auctions. Of course, in time for me to do the Oxford PBFA fair. Veronica always viewed my book and map selling with just a touch of amusement, but she humored me. Besides, the Old Parsonage was one of her favorite hotels, also. In those days it hadn't yet been gussied up and had quite a different kind of charm. Veronica, forever loyal, liked it even after the renovations. As long as we got a suite facing the inner gardens.

This would be a real holiday for me. I hadn't seen Veronica for some months, not since she and I and Lo Ban spent weeks tracking down Amanda, who had been kidnapped in the flea market outside Bangkok.

That harrowing event still causes uneasiness within me. We had not the slightest clue where Amanda had been taken, nor by whom. Nobody came forward and no ransom was asked. Although we didn't discuss it, we all felt that she had been taken as an act of revenge. And that meant she would be murdered.

Lo Ban took matters into his own hands. He disappeared for a while. He went "inside the scene" as he described it later. Shortly thereafter, powerful Asian underworld figures began disappearing, one by one, and then reappearing, but as limp bodies on the sidewalks. Amanda was released.

We never learned who the kidnappers were, but Lo Ban had just put personal pressure on the nearest powerful crime figures. The otherwise inexplicable deaths of their leaders frightened them and they took action, ensuring Amanda's freedom. Lo Ban and Amanda left Thailand for Hong Kong immediately after her release. They did not want to discuss the matter of the bodies with the police. But Veronica and I stayed on at the Oriental Hotel and let that splendid institution pamper and restore us.

Now, with those adventures seemingly in the distant past, I was again the rare book dealer buying in the English markets and spending wonderful, brisk days with Veronica in the English Cotswolds.

Although I had done surprisingly well earlier, buying in the rooms in London, I worked the Oxford fair. I wasn't really expecting to find much in the higher end, but perhaps... Hope, of course, springs eternal when there's a book fair to view.

My low expectations were being met and I had acquired very little by the time the fair was closing. I was leafing through a pile of manuscript material when I came upon a small pocket diary. It wasn't very old — it was dated 1975 — but it had curious contents. I bought it for two quid.

"Mayan," said Veronica. "Definitely Mayan." She was slightly amused. I was more than a little impressed.

Veronica and I spent the rest of the week eating well and catching up on gossip with some of our companions from the old days. Several were still at Oxford and it was a treat to sip sherry with them once again.

I thought little of the purchase until months later when I brought it to a book fair at which I was exhibiting. I showed it to Lo Ban, who expressed immediate interest in his own peculiar way.

"Have I ever told you the story," Lo Ban asked me during a lull in the book fair, "of that curious adventure with Arturo Monages?"

There had been far too many lulls in the book fair and each one had elicited a story from Lo Ban that began with "Have I ever told you..." But I was willing to listen. Anything was better than the sheer and utter boredom of just sitting there, or even getting up to go to the booth down the aisle that had the little dish of hard candies. The dealers there were getting pissed at me and were about to say something snide about the number of candies I was eating. At least they were trying hard to think of something snide, but they had not wit enough to be snide.

Lo Ban leaned back in his chair and assumed that placid countenance that always signalled the onset of a story.

"Monages was a paleographer, interested in Mayan glyphs." Lo ban began to spin the antecedents. "He also collected Burmese horoscopes, but that's another story. Anyway, Monages used to buy a lot of the Burmese manuscripts from me (Lo Ban neglected to mention that these were the same manuscripts that *he* bought from me. So that's where he was flogging them!) and I got to know him well. One day he and I were having dinner in New York. We were in one of those Japanese restaurants on First Avenue in the 30s. The ones that come and go like petals on the reflecting pool."

Lo Ban gloated over this simile. I smiled, trying not to appear bored by yet another one of his interminable stories.

"We were both pigging out on sushi. I was on my third sake and was not paying too much attention to the comings and goings of the people in the restaurant. Monages was feeling no pain. He loved sake. You know, Manasek, I am getting soft in my old age. Never before would this have happened. Never! Then, suddenly two goons come in and start shooting. My old training came through and I got Monages on the floor and pulled the table down over us. The goons ran away and nobody knew for certain what they were after. But Monages knew."

"And that was...?" I asked.

"Monages himself. They wanted to kill him." Lo Ban spoke softly. "They wanted to kill Monages."

I knew Monages a bit and could not imagine why anyone would want to kill him. A slight chap, mild mannered and with a wonderful Zapata moustache, Monages was a very gentle man. A scholar who studied ancient civilizations of his homeland as well as having a keen interest in the products of other cultures, such as the curious kind of divination or horoscope manuscripts he collected. And he was targeted for death.

"But who would want to kill Monages?" I had trouble with this one.

"Veronica was right," said Lo Ban, "when she identified this stuff as Mayan." He pointed to my little manuscript. "This seems to be a copy of parts of a Mayan text."

I knew a little about Mayan texts. They were wonderful books filled with glyphs. Apparently, shortly after the Spanish conquest, Spanish priests destroyed most of the Maya's literature and only bits remained. These treasures are the only written documents of the Mayan culture and civilization extant. Except for the stone carvings, of course.

"Monages was working on the translations. That, of course, was about the time we were beginning to be able to read the things. There was a lot of excitement, especially when a previously unknown text was discovered in a small church in the mountains."

It seemed, according to Lo Ban, that this text had been hidden centuries ago and then forgotten. It was only discovered when the authorities came to arrest the local priest. Apparently they didn't like some of his sermons. The police found the priest hiding in a pile of rubble in an anteroom. The text was found in the rubble. The priest was executed.

"As usual, " continued Lo Ban, "the locals didn't know anything about this book and it was sold for a pittance in the market to a tourist. An American tourist. He made the

mistake of showing his find to his tour guide, who, recognizing the piece's value, slit the tourist's throat and stole the thing."

This story was getting a bit bizarre, even for Lo Ban. "And I suppose Monages got the text from the guide?" I asked.

"Only indirectly," said Lo Ban. "The guide was caught — it doesn't do to kill tourists — and Monages bribed the police to get the manuscript. He justified the bribe on the basis of saving the Mayan manuscript for posterity. The guide had hanged himself in prison while awaiting trial and the police would probably have destroyed the work."

"So now we have the book in safe hands."

"Right," replied Lo Ban. "And if the book had merely been another ecclesiastical text, all would have been well. However, it was very unusual — it listed great treasure and showed where it was hidden. Essentially it was an atlas of Mayan treasure maps. And Monages could read it."

"But it didn't show actual maps?"

"Maps in the Maya culture were not the familiar maps that we know and sell. These were maps, all right, but in a very different format. And they were treasure maps. In a curious way, this was a real atlas."

"So whose treasure is it?"

"Evidently Monages'."

I had trouble with that position. It was Monages' manuscript, sort of, but the treasure was not. "What a dilemma," I thought, as the scene unfolded.

"I was in Guatemala, showing Monages some of my Thai manuscripts, when we decided to take a quick look at one of the treasure sites. Monages had translated part of his atlas and could locate one of the sites on a modern map. It was only a few hours away."

"And?"

"Bingo! We hit the jackpot right away. Exquisite emeralds and gold. Not a lot, but the quality was wonderful. Monages and I turned the site over to the national museum, but they wanted to prosecute us for robbing the find! At that point I left the country. Monages was jailed, but only briefly, and he left as soon as he was released. Meanwhile, word about the find had leaked out. Somehow. Then, some Spanish antiquities dealers put together a consortium to get the atlas from Monages and loot the sites. But the atlas was back in Guatemala, Monages was not about to go back for it, and besides, he had no interest in the Spanish deal."

"And where was I when all this was going on?" I felt a bit annoyed because we usually kept each other advised about things such as this.

"In Istanbul. With Elizabeth. And instructions not to be bothered."

"Amanda and I went back to Guatemala," continued Lo Ban, "but the atlas had disappeared. All that we could find were Monages' notes on the translations. When we brought them back to him, here in the States, he found they weren't enough to locate the other troves. A key set of notes was missing."

"So who would want to kill him?"

"I don't know," said Lo Ban quietly, "and neither does Monages. But the amount of treasure pinpointed in that Mayan atlas is enormous. Any number of groups could be after it."

Perhaps it was only coincidence, perhaps it was destiny. Lo Ban's story was interrupted when two men, visitors to the fair, came over to us, apologized for interrupting us, but "Could they please see that manuscript."

They pointed to the little Mayan glyph notebook that Lo Ban still had, open, in his lap.

Lo Ban looked at them and said "It isn't mine. It belongs to my colleague here."

I was intrigued and handed the book to the fair-goers. "I'm sorry, you can examine it, but it isn't for sale. I was just showing it to my friend."

"We want to buy it. How much?" The question was asked after a very brief conference in Spanish.

"I am sorry, but it is not for sale." I answered them in Spanish.

In response, one of them suddenly pushed me against a nearby bookcase, knocking it, as well as me, over. I was covered in a rain of books. The other man, holding the manuscript, started to run out the door. But he hadn't counted on Lo Ban. With a speed that belied his age, Lo Ban had him on the floor and the would-be thief was writhing with the pain of a badly damaged patella.

Of course, the cops were called. "Anybody wanna press any charges?" asked the police, politely.

"No, it was a simple misunderstanding." We all agreed to act friendly and as though it was all a big accident. Meanwhile, Lo Ban had snatched the manuscript and hidden it deftly. The two left, one limping very badly, and Lo Ban could not resist waving a friendly "good-bye."

"We will see you again." An unfriendly response.

"I have no doubt about that," Lo Ban observed. "No doubt whatsoever."

I glanced at my little notebook again. Lo Ban silently pointed to a very small, discrete gold initial imprinted on the spine. "AM"

"It's Arturo Monages' diary with the missing glyphs. I just noticed the initials when those two guys came by."

When the fair was over we contacted Monages. He recognized the description of the little book and confirmed that it was indeed his, and that it had the missing notes he needed to decipher the rest of his glyphs. He had also made a decision. Would we help him find the sites?

Lo Ban and I looked at each other. Our old group would come out of retirement once again. We didn't have to speak it. We knew.

Snake[1]

The monster said, "It is useless for you to resist; I am going to devour you." But the prince answered, "You may think that I have used all my weapons and am helpless, but I still have one weapon left. If you devour me, I will destroy you from the inside..."

— *The Teaching of Buddha*

I never tire of Bangkok, this Venice where people sing their language and where anything is for sale. There are thousands of industrious little manufactories making all sorts of parts, machines, jewelry, artifacts. Here, in this city, some of the world's great silks can be had, in expensive salons or in simple shops. All prices negotiable. Extraordinary art: ancient Buddha heads made yesterday, great bronzes, some ancient, some made yesterday and hardly distinguishable. Ancient porcelains and pottery, some made yesterday, but hardly discernible from the truly ancient ones, some of which were made yesterday or many centuries ago. Authentic old manuscripts and illustrated texts abounded and, in years past, could be found in the most unexpected places. A simple American GI on R&R or a Japanese businessman on a sex tour could get any pleasure or adventure or disease any time of day or night. On Buddha's birthday, the whorehouses might open a bit

1. Although set in Thailand for the purposes of narration, the events related here took place elsewhere. It would be imprudent to reveal the actual location.

later, say at 10 AM, but nothing like religion or philosophy would interfere with the business of sex in any of its various forms.

It was here, in the "Venice of Asia" that Lo Ban had asked us to meet him. He was his usual mysterious self and did not explain, but we all knew each other well enough to understand that such requests were serious and not to be ignored.

And that is why, that time, Veronica and I were sitting in the Bamboo Bar of the Oriental Hotel savoring their exquisite martinis. We had arrived in Bangkok almost a week ago and were happy playing, relaxing, and letting the wonderful Oriental Hotel take care of us. We still did not know why Lo Ban wanted to meet us here, but we were reasonably certain it wasn't urgent or dangerous.

"I want to share something with you," was all his message had said.

Needless to say, I wasn't unhappy about being here. The weather was, for the season, delightful, and I enjoyed being with Veronica again. Our old group had spread across the planet in recent years and we rarely saw each other.

Also, to Veronica's amusement, I was doing a bit of business. For decades I have bought and sold *Kammavacas*. Among the writings of the world, these heavy lacquer sheets, serving as Buddhist ordination texts, bearing the richly written dark sensuous calligraphy, are very attractive. The lacquer leaves are made up by layering the liquid lacquer over rectangles of cotton cloth, allegedly from the discarded robes of Buddhist monks. For centuries, such ordination texts have been accumulating in monastic libraries and only occasionally released, volume by volume, to the rest of the world.

As a parallel business, I buy and sell other examples of paleography from this region, especially the wonderful incised copper plates and the more ephemeral divination manuscripts on khoi paper.

Veronica found my commercial ventures amusing, remembering how it all began, decades ago, during a cold winter in Oxford. Now, she would arch an eyebrow when the subject was raised, and sometimes she allowed herself a deep, throaty chuckle.

"You're my big wonderful shopkeeper!"

Compliments aside, we were pleased to see Lo Ban and Amanda when they arrived.

"All right, Lo Ban," I asked after dinner, "why are we here?"

Lo Ban leaned back and savored his brandy. "Manasek, I need to show you something. Something that I have kept within me for years and I still do not understand it. You are Christian. You explain it to me."

We did not argue with him. Veronica and I would let the scene play.

Two days later we were driving through the dense jungle of northern Thailand, near the Burmese border. Our ancient Land Rover creaked and groaned, and we were being thrown around on the uncomfortable slab seats. My head hit the unpadded roof each time we went into a rut and once again each time we left the rut. And Lo Ban drove like a maniac. Until he came to a bend in the rutted road, just before it entered the village.

The village was poor. But there was something other than the deep, pervasive poverty that set it apart. To this day, I cannot fully describe the affect of the inhabitants. They seemed to suffer a profound sorrow, some damage to their inner self that had changed them forever. Perhaps it was a shame, or some collective guilt or stigma that had been visited upon them.

"You see it too, then, old friend." Lo Ban answered me sadly when I commented on my observation. "Let me show you something."

We got out of the Land Rover and, still shaky from the ride, Amanda, Veronica, and I followed Lo Ban down a narrow path into a small clearing. The village children, somber little folk, had followed us for a short way, but then dropped back. We were alone. Alone with silence. There was no forest noise and there was no people noise. We felt that we, too, should be silent, and it was only with effort that I spoke.

"Lo Ban, what is this place? What is this thing up ahead?"

We had stopped before a big metal cage with two rooms. Rusted and uncared for, the cage stood in a small clearing. There was lush jungle at the edge of the clearing, but only a low, scrub grass around the cage, as though nothing of significance could grow near it. It seemed that even the jungle growth stayed back.

I noted that each room had a small outside door, also of iron bars and the entire outer wall of the cage, including the doors, was covered with a stout wire mesh, completely covering the cage. The wall between the two rooms was made of vertical bars only, perhaps ten inches apart. The floor was made of wire mesh.

We stood in a silence that was broken by Lo Ban's soft voice.

"About 50 or 60 years ago this region was plagued by a crime wave. Japanese troops had deserted and came here to hide. They pillaged, raped, and behaved badly. It was like an infection. Soon many of the villagers, previously peaceful, became brigands and thugs. The village elders did not know what to do until one of them remembered an ancient remedy.

"The town artificers were set to work building this cage. It took months. Remember, this was and still is a poor village and the ironwork must have cost the village at least a year's collective income. Then they sent teams of hunters into the jungle to catch the largest constrictor they could find. Yes, a snake. Because the outside of the cage was covered with mesh, Snake could not escape. But there were only bars between the two rooms. And Snake could pass between, easily when hungry and skinny, but not after a big meal.

"Anyone convicted of a crime would be put into one of the cage's rooms — the one not currently occupied by Snake. The prisoner would be fed and watered but given no other outside assistance. Snake would only receive water. When Snake became slender enough, he would be able to wriggle between the bars separating him from the convict and feed. After eating, Snake could not fit between the bars, and so was imprisoned in the former convict's room. Meanwhile, if the town had another convicted prisoner, he would be placed in the now-vacant room and maintained until Snake was slender enough to repeat the process, each time alternating cage rooms."

We stood in wonder. It was hard to imagine the horror that went on in this little cage.

"It was a uniquely terrifying punishment. If Snake had just fed, a convicted man might have to spend several weeks in his room until Snake came for him. During these weeks, he would watch Snake grow slimmer, and more menacing each day. Naked but for a loincloth, the convict had no way to defend himself. He did not even receive his meager daily food on a dish or in a cup. He had nothing. And day by day he watched Snake, who, in turn, watched him.

"As Snake grew slimmer and the time of his next feeding grew closer, crowds would gather to watch. The poor wretch within generally went insane, alternately pleading for mercy and lapsing into a stupor.

"Sometimes, when there were two prisoners, or, as it came to be, when the village needed a spectacle, two or more convicts were placed in the same cage. Even so, they were no match for Snake, who would devour them, one by one, in a very unpleasant and widely watched drama. It got so that crowds from neighboring villages would come to watch the final hours. It was a source of profit and the town began to prosper. A prosperity owed to Snake and to a ready supply of criminals.

"The effect of this punishment was dramatic. The sentence was a great deterrent. Crime of all sorts was virtually wiped out in the village and in the whole general vicinity. Peace again settled in and the village, now free of brigands and robbers, prospered. However, with peace and prosperity came another problem that had not been anticipated. Even with the most assiduous law-enforcement, there were now too few prisoners to maintain Snake. Snake had become a liability, for he had to be fed, and this required using local pigs. And Snake was used to being fed well.

"About ten years ago, the village decided to sell its services. Or rather, the services of Snake. It began to take in convicts. Individuals convicted of capital crimes, even in relatively distant areas were carted in and put into the cage with Snake. Soon political prisoners were being used. It must have been like the old days in Paris with the Mob howling for the guillotine. A few years ago I came through here a day after Snake had fed and there still were boisterous mobs walking about the town.

"Then came the case of X. This hapless lad was arrested with about a dozen Rolex watches in his possession. Unfortunately, some of them bore inscriptions identifying their owners, who had been killed by the Khmer Rouge. But the fellow was just a lad of about 12, he knew nothing about the watches. He only knew that he was being paid to carry them down to Bangkok.

"It didn't matter. He was convicted, rather hastily, of murder and sentenced to death. His own village disowned him and quickly agreed to his punishment. Snake.

"I think it was pretty clear to most people that he was just being used as part of a spectacle. But it didn't matter. The young lad was pushed, weeping, into the empty room next to Snake. For almost a week he begged, wept and pleaded. He lost control of his bowels and began banging his head against the bars, but to no avail. Snake was getting thinner and the crowds thicker. The town had become caught up in yet another execution.

"Snake had almost gotten through a few times; soon it would be over. The lad screamed himself hoarse and clung like a monkey to the barred roof.

"But then something else happened. The boisterous crowd that had gathered to watch the approaching end suddenly fell silent. It parted to admit a stooped figure in the robes of a Jesuit priest. Without saying a word, the priest walked slowly with great dignity, as well as with the difficulty of age, to the barred cage. In front of the boy's room, he knelt down and held up his crucifix. The filth-encrusted wretch crept toward him on all fours. Facing each other through the bars, man and boy; priest and doomed, began to pray. Neither spoke the other's language but together they prayed.

"Snake came forward, too. And the three of them formed a tableaux for several hours. A few of the villagers shouted obscenities at them and some hurled dung. But soon they drifted away, skulking. I don't know if they were spooked or if they were shamed. But go away they did.

"A few returned the next day, probably out of curiosity."

"And...?" I asked weakly.

"And, they saw the old Jesuit still kneeling outside. Next to him, outside also, was the boy, holding the crucifix and still praying. But Snake was gone, free again.

"When they approached him, they saw that the Jesuit was dead.

"Remarkably, the cage had been undisturbed; there were no holes and the doors were still locked. The crowd

140

went crazy. It dragged the old priest's body through the streets in a mad frenzy. The mob then grabbed the boy, who was still clutching the crucifix, and dragged him through the streets. He was spat upon and beaten until he finally died. Still with his crucifix. It truly was a howling mob, completely out of control.

"Except for a few. They tried to stop it but were not heard. Pushed aside, they were lucky to escape with their lives. It was they who told me the story. They live with a shame known to few others.

"And the people in this village were never the same again."

My throat was dry. "Why do you come back here?" I could not understand Lo Ban's continued interest in this happening.

"It is a pilgrimage, Manasek. There is something profound here. I cannot forget it. You need to know of it, and I need to share it."

Veronica and Amanda wept silently. Lo Ban and I stood there, creating in our mind's eye that somber scene. Priest, innocent, and Snake.

We returned to the Land Rover. The town's single street was entirely deserted when we drove through on our way back. Our entire return trip to Bangkok was a quiet, somber one. We were all weighted down with the memory of that town, that cage and Lo Ban's story. None of us spoke much during the entire trip.

The four of us were at dinner, two days later, back in Bangkok. Our moods were still somber. We had not been able to rid ourselves of what we had seen and learned. It festered and intruded into our thoughts. That night, eating in a quiet corner of Lo Ban's favorite restaurant, I noticed a tear on Amanda's cheek.

"My friends," I said, as Lo Ban, Veronica, Amanda, and I held hands, forming a ring around the table.

Holy Mary, Mother of God, pray for us sinners now and at the hour of our death...

Colophon

This book was set in the Adobe Caslon family of typefaces.
It was manufactured in the United States of America.

The artwork was done by
Carrie Fradkin, of Norwich, Vermont

Proofreading by Alan Berolzheimer.
Tom Suárez' critical reading helped me enormously.

J'ai vu le soleil bas, taché d'horreurs mystiques
Illuminant de lons figements violets,
Pareils à des acteurs de drames très–antiques.

— Arthur Rimbaud *Le Bâteau ivre* 1883